Romances
by Jennifer Ashley

Riding Hard
ADAM
GRANT
CARTER
TYLER
ROSS
KYLE
RAY

Shifters Unbound
PRIDE MATES
PRIMAL BONDS
BODYGUARD
WILD CAT
HARD MATED
MATE CLAIMED
PERFECT MATE
LONE WOLF
TIGER MAGIC
FERAL HEAT
WILD WOLF
SHIFTER MATES (ANTHOLOGY)
MATE BOND
BAD WOLF
WHITE TIGER
(AND MORE TO COME)

GRANT

RIDING HARD
BOOK 2

JENNIFER
ASHLEY

Acknowledgments

Many thanks go to my editor, Traci Hall, who went above and beyond the call of duty helping me get this book ready for release. Her input and assistance was invaluable.

Thanks also go to my husband, for patiently taste testing chili recipes until we found one that was just right. He prefers the hottest version, of course. He insisted on trying several batches of the cookies too.

Finally, thank you to all the readers who wrote to me with enthusiasm about this new series and encouraged me to continue. More to come!

Chapter One

Christina slid two beers across the bar's top, barely paying attention when the customers told her to keep the change. She didn't notice anything—not the hot, swirling air, the thumping music, or the laughter of the patrons relaxing on a Friday night.

He wasn't supposed to be here.

Grant Campbell strolled in, the cocky, arrogant hotter-than-hell cowboy Christina had tried, and failed, to stop thinking about for the last year or so. He took off his black hat as soon as he walked through the door—he always removed his hat when he went inside anywhere—he was polite that way. He wore a button down shirt, which was formal for a man who lived mostly in T-shirts, but tonight was a special occasion.

His jeans stretched over thighs made tough with riding and stunt work, his walk graceful from the same. The dimmed lights brushed his dark hair, which in the sunlight had highlights of gold.

He didn't come in alone. Grant was never alone. He'd have women with him, usually more than one.

Tonight, it was three. Two wore their hair long; one had cropped it short. All wore jeans that might slide from their slim hips any second, tops that were so tight they might have been painted on.

They were beautiful, of course, in that blond, smooth-faced Texas way. Why was it that every woman who followed Grant around was a walking cliché?

Except Christina. She had black hair that curled and would never lie straight, a body with more cushioning than she liked, and her dad's nose. *You're a Farrell, honey,* her dad liked to say. *No denying it.* He said it proudly, because he loved her, but Christina had long ago realized she'd never be petite.

The girls with Grant were shrimpy. Skinny, except for breasts that couldn't be real. No woman was a perfect right angle like that.

The young women hung on him, fighting for which two would have his arms around them. Grant was grinning, the idiot, loving the attention. Christina slammed used beer mugs two patrons had left into the dirty dish tray, pretending she was way too busy to notice.

Grant got the buckle bunnies to settle down at a table, then turned to approach the counter.

He stopped between one beat and the next, his blue eyes stilling as his gaze fell on Christina. Christina glanced down, rubbing away at the rings the mugs had left. Grant hesitated, poised to turn around and go. He hadn't realized she'd be here tonight.

Then he came on. Grant didn't lose his smile, didn't look the least apologetic. He was well-loved in Riverbend, this was Friday night, and this was Riverbend's only bar. He had every right to be there.

Christina could have turned aside and let Rosie wait on him. She could have slipped out to the tables she was watching, as if she never saw him. Instead, she made herself turn from her wiping and give him a neutral look.

"Hey, Grant. What can I get you?"

His eyes flickered. Christina would not— *absolutely would not*—think about how he'd turned around those words seven years ago to get her to first go out with him.

What can I get you?

You, he'd said with a grin. *Or your phone number. Or you meeting me at the coffee shop tomorrow.*

Christina got propositioned every night, often with similar phrases. But Grant had turned on his Campbell charm, his beautiful blue eyes warm, and Christina had fallen hard.

She'd known Grant and his brothers most of her life. She'd gone to school with him, but he was three years younger, and she'd barely noticed him.

In the time between high school and his first legal entrance into Sam's Tavern, Grant had sure grown up. He'd become tall, deep-voiced, hard-muscled, and athletic.

In the years following, while Grant and Christina had dated, then moved in together, Grant had grown up even more. Now he was a hot, tight-bodied man—successful, handsome ... And he still had that kick-ass grin that had every woman in River County falling at his feet.

The frozen moment passed. Christina saw Grant pretend to relax, though the hand he rested on the counter curled to a fist. "Four beers. Whatever's on tap. Oh, make one of them a light."

"Watching your weight?" Christina asked as she lifted four mugs between her fingers, arranged them in front of her, and positioned the first one under the tap.

Grant didn't answer. "What are you doing here tonight?" he asked. "Thought it was Bailey's bachelorette party. Male strippers and everything." He didn't meet her gaze when he said *male strippers.*

"Starts later. I came in to help out a little." Christina thumped one beer down in front of Grant, swiftly wiping up the foam that spilled out. "What about you? It's Adam's bachelor party tonight too."

Grant shrugged. "Heading there. My friends got thirsty."

Christina didn't reply, especially since one of his "friends" now sauntered up to lean beside him. She was the short-haired one, and had big green eyes framed with so much mascara Christina was surprised her eyelids didn't gum together.

"We're always thirsty," the young woman said, giving Christina a confident smile. "Keeping up with Grant is exhausting."

Grant's and Christina's gazes met. Christina saw Grant's eyes soften and stop short of rolling. He knew the girl was a bubblehead, and he knew Christina knew it too.

Christina and Grant shared a tiny moment, the two of them connected, the deep friendship they'd formed long ago showing itself for a brief space of time.

The glass at the tap overflowed and the moment broke. Christina snapped the handle up, poured out the excess foam, and shook the beer off her hand.

"Just one light, right?" She thunked the glass to the bartop and moved the next glass under the light beer tap.

"For me," the short-haired girl said. "I'm trying to lose twenty pounds. I've already lost six."

She eyed Christina as though she waited for her praise. Christina swept her a critical look, and decided that if the woman lost even *one* more pound, she'd be skeletal.

"Good for you," Christina said without inflection.

Grant didn't respond. Christina remembered when he'd once said, *I don't like skinny women. You never know when something sharp is going to jam you in the eye.*

He caught Christina's gaze, and another flicker passed between them.

Grant shoved mugs at the girl. "You take those two back for me, sweetheart," he said. "I'll be right there."

The young woman gave him a sly look. "Better hurry." She sashayed away, raising the glasses at her friends.

"You taking them to Adam's party?" Christina asked as she filled the last mug. "Are they old enough? Maybe I should card them." She knew they were legal—the girls had been in here before—but she couldn't help herself.

"You know me better than that, Christina," Grant said, frowning. "At least, you should."

Christina finished the last beer, printed out his bill, and set it next to him. "No, I don't think I ever did."

Grant's brows slammed together. He pulled his wallet from his back pocket and yanked out a couple of twenties. "Keep the change."

"No." Christina swept up the bills. "I told you before. I don't want tips from you."

Anger sparked deep in Grant's blue eyes. Last fall at the rodeo grounds Christina had worked a booth serving drinks. When Grant had bought some beer then tried to drop a twenty into her tip jar, Christina had yanked out the money and burned it.

"Just keep it," Grant growled. He grabbed the last beers and walked away.

Christina pretended not to watch his very fine ass as she counted out the change and slapped it onto the polished wood. Pretended, but she couldn't take her eyes off him. Every part of him looked good — back *or* front. *Damn it.*

She swung around, snatched up more dirty glasses from the other side of the bar, and nearly threw them into the tray, holding back at the last minute so she wouldn't break anything. Hard to do, because she suddenly wanted to smash every glass in the place.

When she turned back, it was to see Grant sitting at a small round table with all three women more or less on his lap, laughing like maniacs.

Shit.

"Hey, you've got a tip here," a deep voice rumbled at her. Ray Malory's tall body blocked Grant and his sweeties, his hard face softening as she turned to him.

"Yeah." Christina felt a frisson of relief. She ignored the money and rested her arms on the counter. "Haven't seen you in a while."

"Just got back. Championships in Lubbock this week. I told you about that." He'd done more than tell her. Ray had taken her out the night before he'd gone and they'd ended up at her apartment.

"Oh, I know. It just seemed like a long time."

Ray liked that. He gave her a warm look with his green eyes. "If I'd known you missed me so bad, I would have tried to come home sooner."

Christina laughed. "No, you wouldn't. The day you leave a rodeo early is the day you're done."

Ray had to grin. "How about a beer to celebrate? Hurry it up, barmaid. I tell you, the service in this place is terrible."

"You're a shit." Christina felt better as she turned to pour him a beer. At least somebody was interested in talking to her. She didn't have to giggle and jiggle to catch Ray's attention.

The warmth vanished as soon as Grant threw his head back and laughed.

Christina loved the way Grant laughed. He opened himself all the way, no holding back. He was a warm-hearted man, liking everyone, wanting the world to like him. Not a mean bone in him.

Yet, he could fight with the best of them. He didn't take any shit from anyone, and his arguments with Christina had been loud, long, and passionate. The making up afterward had been just as passionate.

One of the young women managed to straddle Grant's lap, and now she took his face in her hands and kissed him on the mouth.

The bottom dropped out of Christina's world. She set the beer down. Ray said something to her, but she couldn't hear. She could only see the young woman with short hair kissing Grant, and Grant's big hands coming around her waist, holding her steady, just as he'd held Christina for so long, never letting her fall.

"Christina."

Christina dragged her attention back to Ray, who wasn't smiling anymore. He'd turned his head to follow Christina's line of sight, then looked at her again, his mouth a grim line.

"Why don't you call me when you're over it?" Ray shoved a bill onto the bar — way over-tipping, as Grant had — and got himself off the stool.

Christina's heart squeezed with remorse. "Aw, come on, Ray. Wait."

"Listen, baby, I don't need to worry about who you're thinking of when you're with me. You give me a call when you decide." Ray swept up his beer and walked away, raising his hand to friends across the room.

"Damn it." Christina forced herself not to look at Grant, but the double-kick of Ray walking away had her gut clenching.

Ray was a good guy — he didn't deserve to be hurt. He was also very attractive, with his dark hair and sinful green eyes.

But in the end, he wasn't Grant. He'd never be what Grant had been to her, and Ray knew it. *Damn, damn, damn.*

"You need to go," the other bartender, Rosie, said to her. Rosie's eyes twinkled. "Your sister's party, remember? Go — have fun. I got this."

"Thanks, Rosie. Here." Christina gave Rosie the tab and money from Ray. "Keep the tip."

Christina signed herself out on the computer, gave Rosie a brief hug, and took up the change she'd left for Grant.

On her way out, she stopped at Grant's table. The short-haired woman, still on Grant's lap, looked triumphant, but the other two were waiting to cut her out. Grant seemed indifferent—if Christina and the rest of the world wanted to watch him with other women, it was their problem.

"You left your change," Christina said to him. She dropped it on the table between the drinks. "Y'all have a good night."

She walked away. If she swayed her butt a little on purpose, gaining the attention of every male in the place, who cared?

Grant sure didn't. Christina's heart ached. They were done, had been done, and there was nothing more to it. She had to get on with her life.

No matter how freaking hard that was going to be.

Chapter Two

Grant had to explain that a bachelor party meant *men only*, and that Callie — the short-haired girl — and her friends couldn't come.

The three ladies made the expected disappointed noises and pouted, but they decided to stay at the bar when Grant left. He doubted they'd sit alone for long.

Grant had come across the young women from San Angelo hitchhiking when he drove into town for the spice he'd run out of for his famous chili, which he was cooking up in Adam's honor. He knew them slightly from the rodeo circuit and figured he'd drive them into Riverbend before they got themselves hurt or worse. Once there, they'd insisted on a drink, and Grant, always the gentleman, obliged.

He hadn't realized Christina would be there tonight. Tomorrow was Adam and Bailey's wedding. Christina should be home with Bailey, trying on dresses or opening presents or drinking shots off a male stripper's body—whatever women did the night before.

But there she'd been, dispensing beers and not holding back with the mockery. She had no use for groupies, and most of the time, Grant couldn't blame her. He'd pretended to have fun with the girls and ignore Christina, but it had been hard.

His ex looking at him with her beautiful eyes and deciding Grant was a fool wasn't easy to take. And the trouble was, he agreed with her.

He drove his pickup back through town and out the other side to the trailer he'd bought on a patch of land down the hill from Circle C Ranch, his family's home.

They were using Grant's double wide for the party tonight, it being large enough for all the poker tables, once he shoved his furniture against the wall. Plus they could flow outside into the fine spring night. Set on a foundation, his trailer had a green lawn and a grove of trees in back on a big piece of land. Plenty of room for barbecuing and just hanging out.

The others had already arrived by the time Grant made it back with his groceries. Adam greeted him with a bear hug, happy.

Grant had never seen Adam so exuberant. Though one side of Adam's face was permanently scarred, his eyes were free of the darkness they'd held since his accident—the last six months had done wonders for him.

No—Bailey Farrell, who'd marry Adam tomorrow, had done wonders for him. She'd picked up the broken-down Adam Campbell and set him on his feet again. Grant would love her forever for that.

Grant's contribution to the bachelor party, besides opening his house, was his famous hotter 'n' hell Texas chili. The heady aroma greeted him as went into the trailer. He'd left Ross, the youngest Campbell and a sheriff's deputy, to tend it. Ross was doing it dutifully, giving the two vast pots a stir after he waved the wooden spoon at Grant when he walked in.

Ross kept his dark hair very short, unlike the rest of them who let their hair get unruly before cutting it. But then, Grant, Adam, Tyler, and Carter were the bad boys of the family, and played Wild West bandits in their trick riding performances. Ross had decided to go into law enforcement rather than the horse business — to keep his older brothers in line, he always joked.

"'Bout time," Tyler sang out from one of the poker tables he was setting up. "Where you been?" Tyler, the best of them at being a bachelor, had taken charge of the food — except for the chili — drinks, and entertainment.

"Had to give some girls a ride into town," Grant said, hanging up his hat and smoothing his hair. "Then I had to have a beer with them — you know, to be polite."

The guys in the room burst out laughing. "Figures," Tyler said.

"What did you do with them?" Carter asked, his hazel eyes softening for the moment. "Making them wait in the truck?"

More laughter. Grant waved away the teasing and headed for the kitchen. "I left them at the bar. I'm sure they'll find something to do."

"Not tonight, they won't," Tyler said. "Everyone's here."

True, Grant's house was filling up with testosterone. It overflowed with Campbell brothers as well as all their friends from town, around the county, and a few from farther than that.

Grant relieved Ross of his duty, broke the seal on the bottle of hot chile powder he'd gone into town for, and measured out the amount. Some more time bubbling, and the chili would be perfect.

Kyle Malory lifted a beer from the cooler and watched Grant give the chili another stir. There was something in Kyle's look Grant couldn't decipher, but he didn't pay too much attention. The Malorys and Campbells had been rivals for years. The Malorys were champion bull riders, and kind of looked down on the Campbells, who were stunt riders. *Doing tricks,* they'd say. *Not real riding.* To which Grant would say *Falling off bulls isn't real riding either.*

But the rivalry mostly stayed friendly, and Adam and Kyle had cleared the air between them about Bailey. Once it became obvious that Bailey and Adam were madly in love, Kyle had bowed out with dignity. Grant had to respect him for that.

Adam and Kyle still weren't best friends, but Adam had made sure Kyle and his brother, Ray, got invited not only to the wedding but the bachelor party.

Grant set down the spoon, got a beer for himself, and made for the poker tables. "Ray coming?" he asked Kyle as they both sat down. He'd seen Ray at the bar talking to Christina, which had bugged the hell out of him. Then Ray had moved off to greet friends, looking like he was settling in.

Kyle made a show of glancing around the room, then shrugging. "Who the hell knows?"

"Huh. Saw him earlier—thought he was coming."

Kyle looked slightly worried, as he'd done ever since the night last October when Ray had been smashed up in an accident, but he quickly masked his expression. "I don't know what the hell Ray does these days."

Grant shrugged, but the statement didn't make him feel better. Ray had been dating Christina off and on for the past year—everyone in town knew that. So Kyle saying he didn't know what Ray was doing tonight annoyed him.

It shouldn't. Grant and Christina hadn't been a couple in a long time, so why would Grant care who she went out with?

But he did. Ray now got to be the one lying with her in the dark, touching her beautiful body, sliding his hands under her full breasts, tasting her mouth ...

Grant tried not to think about it, but it was impossible. Every time Grant saw Ray, he barely resisted the urge to punch the shit out of him.

Tyler lifted his beer bottle and toasted Adam. "To my big brother, Adam, who's sticking his head into the noose tomorrow morning. Trapped forever into a life of shopping for rugs, buying furniture, kitchen appliances ..."

"Didn't you and Mom buy a new stove last week?" Ross yelled at him.

"Shut up," Tyler said. "Here's to Adam. Boldly going where none of his brothers have gone before."

"You mean down on a woman?" someone called.

Tyler gave him the finger. Adam stood up and raised his own beer.

"Eat your hearts out, losers," Adam said. "I snagged me the best woman in town."

No one could dispute him about that. Bailey was a sweetheart, and Grant had long considered her a good friend. She'd been a friend to him even after Christina broke up with Grant. Adam, his lucky-ass older brother, always landed on his feet.

The party got started. Beer flowed, chili was served. Grant got his usual compliments of *Shit, this is hot – what did the hell did you put in here?* To *You gotta give my dad this recipe, Grant, come on.*

Grant only grinned and told them to piss off. The secret of Grant's chili had been handed down from his grandfather, passed on to only one male Campbell of each generation. He remembered the day his mom had given him a sealed envelope, saying, *You're old enough to have this now.*

Grant had been sixteen, and he hadn't known what to expect from the envelope – the sex talk written down? Secrets to financial success?

He'd been stunned to find his grandpa's chili recipe, written out in his dad's handwriting. Grant had memories of his father standing over the stove, winking at anyone who asked him what he put in the chili and refusing to answer.

The recipe hadn't gone to Adam, the oldest boy. It had come to Grant. Mom had explained that the honor wasn't reserved for the oldest, but the one who would take best care of it. Grant had been very, very proud to be chosen.

Not even his mom, Olivia, knew what was in the recipe. It was a secret that Grant would pass along to his son, when he was ready.

Except it was looking more and more like Grant would never have kids at all. The thought etched sadness into his happiness for Adam.

Grant took a break from the poker table after a while and wandered outside to breathe the clean air of the balmy Texas night. Spring came early in Hill Country, with grasses turning green, and bluebonnets carpeting the sides of the roads and along the streams. Right now, the moon was high, the night cool and clear, but winter's chill was gone.

Tomorrow Grant would stand up—the best he could after a night of pouring beer down his throat—as best man to Adam, the brother he was closest to. He was happy for him, but sad to say good-bye. Adam and Bailey would be heading back to California after their honeymoon in New Orleans, to work together on a movie Adam was the stunt coordinator for.

Bittersweet. That was the term for what Grant was feeling.

"Hey, Grant," Kyle Malory said. He stepped off the small porch and moved down the drive to where Grant stood, taking in the night. "Been meaning to talk to you."

"'Bout what?" Grant remembered Kyle eying him earlier, and faint interest perked through his moroseness.

"My sister."

Grant looked at Kyle in surprise. The Malory girls, Grace and Lucy, were outside the Campbell-Malory feud, by tacit agreement between both families. Grace, the younger sister, lived in Riverbend, while Lucy had moved to Houston a while ago, though she'd returned for the wedding.

"Which one?" Grant asked.

"Grace." Kyle's answer was clipped. "She's been going through a hard time. You heard about her restaurant?"

"Sort of." Grant folded his arms and inhaled sweetly scented night air. "She was going to open it down in Fredericksburg, right? And then something happened?"

Kyle growled. "Yeah, her partner disappeared with all the money, leaving Grace holding the bag." His eyes flashed in the darkness. "If I ever catch up to him …"

Grant nodded, understanding Kyle's anger. "What a bastard."

"Yeah." Kyle's tone said everything it needed to. "Anyway, Grace is taking it hard. Not happy."

"I don't blame her. Is that what you wanted to ask me? To help you track this guy down and kick his ass?" Grant would be happy to tell the man what he thought or maybe hold him down while Kyle did.

"No." Kyle paused. "Although that's not a bad idea. No, what I was getting around to asking is whether you'd take her out. You know, to dinner, or whatever. To make her feel better."

Chapter Three

Grant didn't register the words for a moment or two, then he stopped. "Wait, wait, wait. You want me to *ask Grace out*?"

Kyle shrugged. "Why not? I thought you two were friends."

"We are. But you just asked me to take *your sister* out on a date." Grant slammed his forefinger to his chest. "Me, Grant Campbell."

"Yeah." Kyle looked annoyed. "What's the big deal?"

"Because you've tried to kick my ass before for even *looking* at your sisters."

"Sure." Kyle folded his arms across his chest. "When we were kids."

Grant gave him a narrow glance. "Hold up, Kyle. You never have a change of heart—not you. So why are you trying to fix her up with me? What's this about?"

"I told you, to make her feel better." Kyle gave him a stony look. "She's upset."

"And you think a Campbell taking her out is the solution?"

Kyle unfolded his arms in exasperation. "Shit, if I'd known you'd be so pig-headed stubborn about it, I wouldn't have mentioned it."

It was dark, but Grant could see Kyle avoiding his gaze. Something was going on here, but Grant couldn't figure out what.

"She won't go out with me," Grant said.

"How do you know? You ever asked her?" Fury entered his eyes as he spoke, as though Kyle were adding *You'd better not have.* This was weird.

"I didn't have to. She told me a long time ago she'd never go with me. She said we'd be *Grace and Grant,* and that sounded stupid, so she didn't want us to be a couple. I'm pretty sure she hasn't changed her mind."

Kyle growled. "Fine, then. Don't. Forget I even asked."

"Does Grace know you're trying to set her up?" Grant asked. "I bet she'd kick your ass if she found out. Huh, mine too, probably."

"Well, then don't let her find out." Kyle gave him a belligerent glare before subsiding. "Look, I'm just worried about her. Grace had her heart set on that restaurant. She loves to cook. That jackass took her dream away from her, and now she doesn't even have a job. She could work for Mrs. Ward, but she wouldn't earn very much."

Mrs. Ward ran the only restaurant and bakery in town. "At least she'd be doing what she loved," Grant pointed out.

"Yeah, maybe. But Grace would always be second to Mrs. Ward and her daughters, and she knows it. I wish I could find something for her." Kyle's anger disappeared, leaving him with a worried look.

Grant shrugged. "Tell you what. I'll keep an ear out. But Grace might have to leave Riverbend if she wants to get into the serious chef stuff."

"Yeah, I know. She's talked about going to Houston and staying with Lucy. She won't be happy there, though. She loves it here."

It was Grace's decision, Grant thought, but didn't say so. Everyone had their problems, he guessed.

"Never mind." Kyle returned to his usual brisk manner. "Forget I said anything. I think the stripper's here. We'd better go in and act like we're eighteen or Tyler will get his feelings hurt."

"Tyler's not going to care what we think," Grant said.

"That's true, as long as he gets an eyeful. Come on."

Grant followed, wondering why the hell Kyle had spent twenty minutes trying to convince him to go out with his baby sister. Kyle never did anything without a reason, and that reason was rarely favorable to Campbells.

At least the conversation had shaken Grant out of his self-pity and given him something to think about. He sure needed it.

***

"Go ahead and kiss the bride," the minister said to Adam.

As Christina's already wet eyes brimmed with fresh tears, Adam turned to Bailey, caressed her cheek, and pressed a kiss to her lips.

No one should really whoop in church, but the Campbell boys did it anyway. Even Carter grinned as Tyler, Grant, and Ross made noise, all of them happy for Adam.

Bailey, in her body-hugging white dress, white flowers in her hair, flushed as Adam's kiss deepened. She brought her hand up to cup his neck, and the kiss went on.

Tyler laughed and the church filled with *aws* and whistles. The minister, who was a family friend, said, "Now, now, Adam. Time for that later."

Christina, next to Bailey as her maid of honor, watched her sister with warmth in her heart. Bailey had gone through a long period of stress and misery, until Adam had come home. The pair's feelings for each other had rekindled—more than rekindled. They'd built a bonfire. Adam and Bailey had needed each other; they'd come together and life was good.

Christina's gaze flicked to Grant, who stood with Adam as best man.

Damn, but he looked good. Grant wore a tux, as all the brothers had today, though they'd insisted on cowboy boots. Grant's coat stretched across broad shoulders, the suit hugging his lithe body.

As though he felt Christina watching, he turned his head and looked at her, his eyes so blue in his Texas-tanned face. Their gazes met, and Grant lost his smile.

Should have been us. The words whispered through Christina's mind as though Grant had spoken them. Christina and Grant had lived together a long time before the breakup. They'd have made it permanent if they both hadn't been so angry and stubborn.

And young, Christina thought. *We were too young to be so serious about everything. Stupid decisions made in the heat of youth.*

Grant's mouth set in hard lines and one hand curled at his side. She wondered if he were thinking the same thing.

Grant's brows pinched together. He moved his head the slightest bit, as though shaking it in the negative, and he pulled his gaze from hers. Christina looked away, steel fingers of hurt clamping around her heart.

Adam and Bailey finally stepped apart, neither looking ashamed of their passionate kiss. The minister, now that he had quiet again, pronounced the final blessing.

The organist played a fervent recessional as Bailey turned with her new husband and walked arm-in-arm with him back down the aisle.

Now came the part Christina had been dreading. As maid of honor, she was to take Grant's arm, and let him lead her out.

They hadn't practiced it at the rehearsal— Christina's mother had said, *Then Grant and Christina go out,* but she hadn't made them go through the motions.

Christina had been standing out of the way, in a cluster with the Malory girls. Grant hadn't even looked at her.

Christina's eyes were sandy from the bachelorette party—though she'd avoided the Jell-O shots, she'd done too much rollicking dancing with the guy dressed as a fireman, trying to erase the memory of the blond woman straddling Grant's lap and kissing him. Hadn't worked very well.

The stripper had been *hot* but once his stint was over, he'd simply packed up and gone home. *Probably to his boyfriend,* Lucy Malory had said regretfully.

Grant was looking at Christina now. Blue eyes like summer skies put a lump in her throat the size of a baseball.

He walked stiffly off the step that led to the altar rail and stuck out his arm. Christina, heart beating too fast, lightly put her fingers on his sleeve.

Even that one touch was a mistake. Christina felt the warmth of Grant through his coat, the vibrant power of him through the thin fabric.

Grant's athleticism never ceased to amaze her. He was a large man, with muscles to match, yet he could leap onto and off of a horse with the grace of a big cat. He'd taken falls that would have seriously injured many a man, only to roll away and come up lightly on his feet.

That controlled power came to Christina now through her fingertips. She'd loved running her hands over his beautiful body when they'd lain together in the dark. She'd loved doing it in the heat of the afternoon, and the coolness of the morning.

Grant said nothing at all as he took them swiftly down the aisle after Adam and Bailey. *Going the wrong way,* Christina thought. Rushing away from the altar instead of toward it.

Once they made it outside, Grant moved away from Christina as if he couldn't drop her hand fast enough.

Christina pasted on a smile to cover the ache of his dismissal. The photographer was snapping pictures, and she'd be damned if she'd ruin her baby sister's wedding photos.

They took tons of pictures outside the church — of the bride and groom, the entire wedding party, bride and groom with parents, bride with her attendants, groom with his, all members of both families together.

Adam had more people on his side — four brothers and small Faith, his mom, Olivia, beaming proudly. On Bailey's side, Christina and their mother and father filled the space with warmth. Mom and Dad were so happy for Bailey, and they loved Adam.

"Are we done with pictures?" Adam growled after a time. "My face is going to crack."

"Mine too," Bailey said, rubbing the sides of her mouth.

Christina stepped in front of them. "But you look so cute, Adam." To his glower, she laughed. "No, seriously, you two look awesome."

She hugged them — her sister she loved with all her heart and the cowboy who'd swept Bailey off her feet.

Christina was aware of Grant next to Adam, though she did her damnedest not to look at him. "When do we get to the drinking?" Grant drawled.

"'Cause you didn't get enough of that last night," Tyler said. "You're gonna be in a coma for a week."

Grant shrugged. "What else are weddings good for?"

Adam laughed at him. "I can think of *one* thing." He drew Bailey up to him for a long kiss.

Everyone went *aw*. Faith snapped a picture with her blue spangled phone.

Faith's shot turned out to be Christina's favorite photo of the wedding. Adam was scooping Bailey up with one arm, kissing her in pure joy, Bailey's arm straight down beside her, her hand clutching her bouquet of white roses.

The rest of the family was gathered around, focused on Adam and Bailey, every single one of them smiling or laughing. Christina helped Faith print it out afterward and Bailey framed a copy for everyone.

The reception was held at the Campbells' ranch, the Circle C. Christina rode to it with Bailey and Adam and the Malory girls in the limo. The three unmarried women squished together in one seat, teasing Adam and Bailey, who sat opposite and couldn't stop kissing each other.

While traditionally the bride's parents were supposed to organize the entire day, the Campbells' mom, Olivia, had said, "We have plenty of room—why shouldn't we have the reception at the ranch? Be easier for the Farrells too, coming in from out of town."

Christina and Bailey's parents now lived in San Antonio, where their father worked as an engineer. Close enough that they could drive to Riverbend in a couple of hours, but too far to make planning a wedding convenient. Olivia and Christina's mom, friends from way back, put the whole thing together, with help from Christina, and also Grace Malory, who was one hell of a pastry chef. Her restaurant would have been awesome.

"If we have the reception at the ranch," Faith had said excitedly, "the horses can come too."

The girl was wise enough to realize the horses couldn't attend *literally*, but she was happy that they could watch from corrals or their open stalls in the barn.

A huge white tent went up on the slope behind the house, the path lined with potted flowers and streamers. A barbecue had been set up outside to cook all kinds of food, and champagne and beer came in by the crateload. White ribbons, white roses, and splashes of pink, yellow, and red flowers made everything festive, beautiful, and welcoming.

The party began when the limo deposited them all at the ranch. Christina walked behind the rest of the party as they made their way to the tent, both happy for her sister and sad for herself.

Then came feasting, dancing, celebrating. Grant stood up and gave the best man's toast.

"How the hell my good-for-nothing older brother got so lucky, I'll never know," he said, champagne glass in hand, to the waiting crowd. "I guess he fell on his head enough times to realize he needed to hold on to something good." He waited for the laughter to fade then lifted his flute. "To Adam and Bailey. The best-looking couple in Riverbend."

"It ain't hard to be!" a male voice shouted from the back.

More laughter. Grant went on in a louder voice. "The best-looking and the biggest-hearted. I love you guys."

"To Adam and Bailey!" The toast rang out, most enthusiastically from Christina. She sent Grant a smile — he really could be sweet.

Grant caught her look, flushed dark red, and sat down.

***

As the party went on and dancing began, Christina figured she had two choices. She could hide her pain and make sure Bailey had the best day ever, or she could get drunk with the other girls, make a big fool of herself, and maybe try to get laid.

Christina picked option one. She wasn't much of a drinker and this was Bailey's day. It wasn't about Christina and her stupid, messed-up life.

Everyone in town was there, and a few from out of town Christina didn't know. Adam had invited some of his stuntman friends who were being admired by all the ladies, including Lucy. Carter was walking around with a stranger—a well-groomed woman in a subdued beige silk dress that set off her slender limbs and pretty face. She watched the crowd with interest but stayed with Carter and Olivia, talking quietly to them. Christina noticed other guests eyeing her curiously—they didn't know who she was either.

Ray was there, but he wouldn't look at Christina. He'd avoided her at the church and then at the reception, dancing with everyone but her.

Kyle Malory took Christina to the dance floor once, but mostly he wanted to know what was up between her and Ray. Christina said, "Nothing we really want to talk about," and refused to discuss it. If Ray wanted his brother to know his business, he'd tell him.

By the time the night was well advanced, Christina's head hurt and her throat ached. No, she realized, her entire body hurt, even her face, from keeping up all this damned smiling. She was happy for Bailey, but also exhausted and heartsore.

Grant was ignoring her, which was fine, but did he have to flirt with every woman in the tent? Christina felt guilty about angering Ray, which made her heart ache even more.

She ended up outside in the dark, under the cluster of live oaks not far from the house. The tall trees rustled in the night breeze, the music and laughter from the tent muted in the distance.

Christina took a few breaths of the soft air, letting it calm her. She could do this. She could make it until Bailey and Adam drove off to New Orleans for their honeymoon. She'd kiss her sister good-bye, wish her well, and wave her off.

Then she, her mother, Olivia, and anyone else who could be recruited, would start cleaning up. Put away the party, and go back to real life. Bailey was starting a new journey—Christina had to keep on going with the old.

She sighed. No use standing around being maudlin and depressed. Bailey didn't deserve that.

Christina straightened up and took a step toward the path to the tent ... and was brought to an abrupt halt. Branches of scrub around the trees had tangled in the big pink tulle bow on the back of her dress, and now they held her fast.

"Great," she muttered.

She tugged. Nothing. She tugged harder, and froze when she heard fabric rip.

If she tore the dress trying to get away, Bailey and her mom would not be happy. Not only that, Christina would have to walk around the party with the back half of her dress gone, because all of her clothes were at Bailey's.

"Shit," she whispered.

Christina heard a step on last year's fallen leaves, saw the silhouette of a man backlit against the distant tent. She recognized him in a heartbeat, could never forget his broad-shouldered form, his easy stance.

He must have recognized her in return, because he turned on his heel and started back the way he'd come.

"Grant!" Christina called softly. "Don't walk away. Help me!"

Grant paused, turned, and peered into the shadows. "Christina, what the hell are you doing?"

He stepped beneath the trees, out of the moonlight. Now he was a smudge of white where his tux shirt was, his blue eyes rendered black.

"I'm not doing anything," Christina said. "I'm stuck."

"In the mud?"

"No, to the tree."

It sounded stupid as it came out of her mouth. Grant snorted a laugh.

"What were you doing?" he asked. "Climbing it?"

Christina made a noise of frustration. "I came out here for a breath of fresh air. I've got twigs or something tangled up in the dress."

"Climbing it," Grant said with conviction. "Or climbing someone else. Where's Ray?"

"I came out here by myself. Damn it, Grant. Just help me."

Grant chuckled. "Grace under pressure."

"I suck at that, and you know it. You going to help or just laugh at me?"

"Laughing at you is more fun," Grant said as he came closer. "Hold still."

He worked at the twigs woven through the tulle. Christina didn't move, the warmth of him holding her in place more securely than the branches.

Grant tugged harder, his sleeve brushing her bare back. "You are well and truly stuck."

"I know that."

Grant pulled at the big wad of tulle sewed to the satin. "Maybe I can just remove the bow. Oh, wait, some of the back of the dress is tangled too. You might have to rip the whole thing."

Christina let out an exasperated breath. "Geez, Bailey will kill me. She and Mom spent so much time on the dresses."

"You can always take it off." Grant's tone moved from laughing to sensual as his blunt fingers flicked the tab of the zipper.

Christina stilled as heat rocketed through her. Fire moved from his finger on the zipper down between her legs and up again to her breasts.

An image flashed through her head of Grant skimming the dress from her, his arms around her, she lifting to him, their bodies coming together in the darkness under the trees.

She cleared her throat. "Right," she said, her jaw tight. "And run around in my underwear? I'd look like a fool."

"No," Grant said in a low voice. "That's not what you'd look like."

Christina held her breath. Moonlight caressed Grant's face as he gazed at her for a long moment.

The moment broke and he bent to concentrate on loosening the twigs from the dress.

Christina turned her head to study his jaw, brushed with dark whiskers, the dark hair smoothed around his ear. All she had to do was lean a little farther, and she could take his earlobe between her teeth.

Grant's hand brushed her bare scoop of back, his touch hot and strong. Christina couldn't breathe, couldn't think. A breeze swirled around her and she shivered.

"Ah. Got it."

The dress went slack as the twigs loosened their hold. Christina stepped away from both the tree and Grant.

"Thanks," she said quickly.

He said nothing, so she nodded at him, and started to walk away.

"You got crap all over you," Grant said behind her. "Might want to do something about that."

Christina balled her fists, her heart sinking. She wanted to get away from him before she did something stupid, but she marched back to him as well as her high heels let her. "Brush it off. Please?"

Grant went silent as his warm hands started down the dress, picking things out of the tulle, smoothing the satin.

After a moment, his hands slowed. Grant was standing almost on top of her, his feet alongside hers. Christina's hip moved against his thighs, and then against what was between his legs.

Hard and thick, his cock pressed the fabric of his tux pants, telling her he wasn't immune to their closeness, the intimacy of being alone together in the dark.

Grant's chest moved with his intake of breath. His touch stilled on her back, only to come around her waist as he turned her, pulling her against him.

Christina's hands landed on his chest, fingers curling.

For one heartbeat, two, they looked at each other. The breeze swirled around them, bringing the laughter from the tent, the acrid smoke of the barbecue mixed with the mellow scent of spring wildflowers.

"Aw, fuck," Grant said in a hoarse whisper.

Christina couldn't breathe as Grant's hold tightened on her, and he came down to cover her mouth in a raw, desperate kiss.

Chapter Four

Christina tasted like champagne and smelled like roses. Grant opened her mouth with his, their tongues tangling, seeking, hands dragging each other closer.

Christina's dress molded perfectly to her body, the satin letting Grant run his palms up her waist, under her breasts. Only the tulle got in the way, a huge lump of it where her ass was. But screw it. He could kiss her fine like this, cupping her breast in his hand.

Any second one of them would come to their senses and push the other away. *Any moment now.*

Christina clutched at his jacket, and damned if she didn't start pushing it open. Her hands landed on his cummerbund then moved quickly up the thin shirt. Fingertips found his flat nipples and she started to caress them.

She must remember how much he loved that. Tingling started in Grant's chest and rushed to meet the fire in his already hard cock.

He broke the kiss long enough to slide his confining coat from his arms, letting it fall into the mud — who cared? Christina was already coming up to him as Grant brought his mouth down on hers again.

He kissed her swiftly, needing her. Too long, too long without her.

Grant slid his hands to her thighs as they frantically kissed and shoved her skirt upward. She wore stockings with elastic tops, not pantyhose. *Nice.* Her underwear was a thin band of satin and lace, easy to move.

Grant's fingers found her heat. Warm liquid flowed over his hand, and Christina made a soft sound against his mouth.

The alcohol Grant had consumed floated around in his brain, combining with his loneliness and need for this woman. He slid his fingers inside her and was rewarded with the jerk of her body, the growl in her throat.

"Christina," he whispered against her mouth. "I love how you're always wet for me."

Her answer was to renew the kiss, a crush of lips, her mouth seeking his.

Christina's questing fingers found the latch of the cummerbund and it followed the jacket to the ground. The button and zipper of his tux pants opened next. Christina shoved her way in, and then she was locking her hands around his cock.

"*Damn,* woman."

Christina was sweet and hot, and what the hell had he been thinking, walking away from her?

They were hungry for each other. They always had been.

Christina knew exactly how to make Grant come alive. She knew how to stroke him, how to flick her thumb over his tip, which made him jerk.

He rubbed her in response, and she rocked against his hand, the two of them both giving and taking.

Their kisses were frenetic. Teeth scraped lips, mouths bruised. Christina suckled his tongue. Grant groaned against her as Christina's hands moved on him, exactly matching the rhythm of his fingers inside her.

He was going to come standing up. But what did he expect with this hot, sexy woman in his arms, who knew exactly how to work him?

"You're sweet, baby," he said. "It's always so good, you and me."

Christina was moving against him, her excitement rising. Grant loved how she came—exuberant, totally into it, letting herself go without shame. The anticipation of seeing that again ramped his own excitement high.

"*Grant!*" The bellowing voice of Carter floated up the hill from the tent. "You out here?"

Shit.

Christina tore herself away from Grant, stumbling back before he could catch her. Her hand was gone from his cock, chill wind taking place of her warmth.

Christina shimmied her skirt down and took another step back, breathing hard.

"Damn it." Grant choked on the words, coughed. "My brothers are so effing good at timing."

His pants were sagging around his thighs. He did not need Carter jogging up here, finding him with his slacks falling down and his cock hanging out. Grant pulled up, zipped, buttoned, and then groped on the ground for his cummerbund.

Carter was heading this way, and he had someone with him.

"Christina," Grant said, moving to her. He didn't know if this had been a crazy one-off or a prelude to make-up sex, or the first step at reconciliation. All Grant knew was that he didn't want to let her go. Not if there was a chance for them.

"Go on," Christina said, her voice grating. "Go — he's not going to wait."

Grant stared at her a moment, trying to read her. Her stance said *pissed off*, her breathing and her tone said *scared*. Of what?

Grant lifted his coat, tried to brush it off, gave up, and folded it over his arm. When he looked up to tell Christina to come with him, she was gone.

Where she'd stood was empty moonlight, only a few scraps of pink tulle floating on the grass to say she'd ever been there at all.

"Fuck," Grant said softly, and went to meet Carter.

***

Carter was with a woman Grant had not met, though he'd seen her at the reception. Not a date, he concluded — the woman wore a rather plain beige sheath dress, had blond hair tamed into a soft, pulled-back bun, and wore only a smattering of jewelry on ears and fingers. She was in her thirties, brown-eyed, pretty in that successful-woman kind of way.

Probably a new client, wanting trick riders for some show or one of her horses trained. Carter obviously had invited her to the reception, but Carter was ready to talk business with anyone at any time. He rarely let down his walls.

Besides, Carter didn't date. He'd hook up with a woman, have sex with her, maybe see her a few more times, and that was it. He didn't go chasing them, and never mixed business with sex.

"Grant Campbell?" the woman asked before Carter could speak. "I'm Karen Marvin." She opened her small purse and held out a card. "Casting director for Weldwood Studios. We shoot commercials. I need a cowboy. Maybe three. And someone to put together the riding stunts."

So, a client. Grant rolled the card around his fingers and stepped back so she wouldn't try to shake his hand. With what he'd just been doing, probably not a good idea.

Commercials were usually cast through an agency, who'd contact the Campbells and ask them to come in for an audition. But sometimes people sought out the brothers directly and asked them to set up the whole shoot, plan the stunts, do the riding, and hire extra riders if necessary.

At any other time, Grant would be happy to start working out a new show. Right now, however, with Christina's kisses burning his lips, the imprint of her fingers on his cock, he didn't give a shit about anything but her.

"We were thinking—train robbery," Karen was saying. "A couple of bandits robbing a train, all in a hard day's work."

Grant kept the card going around. Karen looked him up and down, noting his coat over his arm, his rumpled shirt. His hair was probably a mess as well, and if Christina had been wearing lipstick ...

Karen's eyes glinted. She knew damn well what Grant had been doing out there in the dark, and that they'd interrupted him. And she thought it was funny.

"What is this commercial for?" Grant asked abruptly.

Carter answered. "Laundry detergent. Don't ask. I said we could probably do it, but I had to talk about it with you first, since you'd be lead rider."

Carter rode as well, but he spent most of his time making deals, following up with clients, and talking to people who owed the business money. People forked out what they owed quick when they saw Carter coming to talk to them. Though no longer the degenerate teen, Carter could be damn scary.

"A train robbery," Grant said. "Means we'll need a train."

"Taken care of," Karen answered, one hand on her hip. "There's a historical society that restores trains nearby and we'll be hiring one, plus an engineer to drive it."

Grant had heard of them, but he'd never been out there. "Then I'll need to take a look at the place." Grant ran his hand through his hair, hoping to tame it down. "Talk to them, figure out what kinds of things we can do, make sure we can do everything safely. The whole bit."

"I'll leave that to you," Karen said. "Do we have a deal?"

Grant looked at Carter, and Carter gave him the faintest nod. Meant the money was good enough to go for it, and that they'd have plenty of control.

Grant knew Carter had already decided before bringing Karen to meet Grant. He was just being polite.

"Sure," Grant said, shrugging. "I don't see why not. Leave the stunt set-up to me. Tyler is one of the best riders there is, and I can bring in a couple other guys, depending on how many you need."

"Good." Karen put warmth in the word. She looked at Carter, then at Grant again, and repeated, "Good," with a hint of sensual interest.

She was enjoying standing between two cowboys, Grant realized. Liked having men around her, especially ones in good shape who might be interested in taking her to bed. Grant should tell her not to pin her hopes on Carter, and she shouldn't pin her hopes on Grant either. Now that he'd had another taste of Christina, Grant wasn't about to move on to anyone else.

"Nice reception," Karen said, as though she had nothing else on her mind. "Thanks for letting me come, Carter. I hope I didn't intrude." She shot Grant another knowing look.

"Nah," Grant said. "Our mom invited the whole town. Couldn't have you be the only one sitting alone in the motel."

"I'm staying in Fredericksburg," Karen said. "Cute place, so historic."

She was a city girl, Grant surmised. They didn't like being out in the country unless it was tamed and manicured and close to a metropolis.

"Long way to drive, this late," Grant said.

Carter nodded. "Maybe you should stay at the house." Generous, for Carter, who didn't like strangers anywhere near his family.

Karen gave a brief laugh. "Thanks, boys, but I'm a big girl. Good at taking care of myself. I wouldn't mind, though, if you walked me to my car, Mr. Campbell," she said, sending Grant a suggestive look. "It's dark, and I'm a bit turned around, so if you could point the way out of town ..."

Grant did *not* want to escort this woman anywhere — why the hell couldn't Carter? Grant was far more interested in finding Christina, talking to her ... All right, kissing the hell out of her again. But his mama had raised him to be polite.

Grant held out his arm, trying not to sound resigned. "Sure," he said. "Come on."

Chapter Five

Karen held on to Grant's arm as they walked away from Carter, but only to steady herself through the wet and clumpy grass. No clutching or crushing her body into his, as the groupies did. Simply walking along as though they were old friends.

The guests' cars had been parked in the circular drive in front of the house, excess vehicles spilling into the field beyond. No one was out here right now — everyone was still dancing and partying in the tent. In the driveway and field, all was darkness and silence.

"I *did* interrupt you, didn't I?" Karen asked, glancing up at Grant. "Sorry about that."

"Nah, it was ..." Grant cleared his throat. "It wasn't going anywhere."

"Too bad." She sounded genuinely sympathetic. "Weddings can be hell. You get bored, so you hook up, and both of you are too drunk to realize it's a bad idea. Then it's awkward when you see each other again."

"Sounds like you go to a lot of weddings."

"No, honey, I was talking about one of *mine*." Karen cackled with laughter. "My first one. That groomsman was too hot to pass up. But hey, my husband was running after my maid of honor, so what the hell? Both of us knew in our hearts the marriage wouldn't last."

"Then why did you go through with it?" Grant asked, mystified. Seemed like a lot of trouble for nothing.

Karen moved her hand in an indifferent gesture. "I was seriously young, and I sort of believed in happily ever after. I thought the magic ring on my finger would make it real. He probably did too. After my third husband—the vile, cheating bastard—I finally realized that there's no such thing as happily ever after. There's only happy for now." She stopped. "Oh, no offense. I mean, your brother and his new wife might be one of the lucky ones, who knows? They do make a cute couple." Karen rubbed Grant's arm, her interest in cowboys coming through the caress. "Where do you stand on happily ever after, Mr. Campbell?"

Grant shrugged, though his heart was beating thickly. "I don't know. I guess it happens, but not to everyone."

"Ah, you're wise for one so young."

Grant would be twenty-eight this year. Christina was thirty now, and this woman couldn't be much older than her.

"Where you from?" Grant asked with genuine curiosity.

"I live in Houston for the moment, but originally from Los Angeles. Got into filming young, and realized that it's cheaper to shoot in places other than California. Lots of studios in Canada these days, for instance, and New Mexico."

"Yeah, we do some work in New Mexico. Arizona too." Grant's mouth kept up the conversation, while his mind was back under the trees with Christina. "You can still find the Wild West out there."

Karen stopped him next to a four-door BMW. "You ever do any acting outside of stunt work?" she asked. "You look good. I've seen some of your performances — the camera obviously loves you."

People asked him this all the time. Grant had long ago come to terms with what he was good at, and what he wasn't. "Trouble is, I can't act. Give me lines, and I get all uptight. I blow every take. If I stick to riding, not talking, I'm fine."

"I don't know about that." Karen didn't touch him, but she looked him up and down. "With the right coaching, you could do something. Let me think about it." Karen took keys from her pocket and clicked a remote. Her car chirped, and lights blinked. "Looking forward to working with you, Mr. Campbell."

She opened the car door then turned and stuck out her hand. Grant still didn't want to touch anyone, but people got offended when you didn't shake hands with them. He grabbed her by the shoulder instead and dropped a quick kiss to her cheek.

"It's Grant," he said. "Mr. Campbell was my dad."

Her smile shone out. "All right, then, Grant. Good night."

"Good night. Drive careful, now."

Karen slid gracefully into her sleek sedan. "I will. Sweet dreams." She closed the door, started the car, gave him a last wave through the window, and pulled away.

She'd indicated before that she needed directions, but she didn't seem to need them now. Karen maneuvered her car slowly around the other vehicles, then headed down the long drive and turned right at the end, which was the way to go for the highway to Fredericksburg. Asking for directions had been a pretense to get Grant to walk her to her car.

Oh, well. Grant got propositioned by women all the time. He wasn't egotistical enough to think it was because he was the greatest guy ever. The buckle bunnies wanted to sleep with the stunt-riding cowboy, and didn't really care what Grant was like as a person. He'd come to terms with that long ago too.

Grant hiked back toward the house. He was only glad Karen hadn't propositioned him to do it right there in the back of her car. He'd have had to refuse, she might have canceled the deal, and Carter would have been pissed off.

But Grant only wanted to find Christina. So he could ... what? Continue where they left off?

Or apologize for the make-out session—hell, why should he? He wasn't sorry. And it wasn't like Christina hadn't been climbing all over him. That had been a mutual, desperate groping.

Halfway down to the tent, he met Carter coming up the path, heading for the house, a sleeping Faith in his arms.

"Karen gone?" Carter asked him in a low voice.

Grant nodded. "Yeah, she's fine." He too kept his voice down so they wouldn't wake Faith. "You seen Christina around?"

Carter gave him a once-over, taking in the mess that was Grant. "No, I haven't."

His gaze went to Grant's coat over his arm, which Grant realized had mud all over it. He couldn't put it back on—anyone seeing him would have a pretty good idea how he'd mucked it up.

"Take mine," Carter said. "I've already said good-bye to Adam. I'm not going back."

He held out Faith, who was sound asleep. In her satin flower girl's dress, a miniature of Christina's, tulle bow and all, she looked adorable.

Before Grant could reach for her, another flutter of satin pushed past him. Grace Malory, who'd been hurrying up the path, held out her arms for Faith.

"I'll take her, Carter," she said. "Poor little thing is worn out."

"Thanks." Carter passed off his daughter to Grace. Faith remained limp, completely trusting. "If she wakes up, tell her I'll be right there."

"Will do." Grace flashed Carter a warm smile before carefully carrying Faith up the path and into the house.

Carter stripped off his coat and handed it to Grant.

Grant took it absently. What he'd seen in Grace's glance explained the weird request by Kyle that Grant ask his sister out. Kyle must have noticed the way Grace looked at Carter, and decided that if Grace had to throw herself away on one of the Campbell family, better it was Grant than Carter.

The realization pissed Grant off. Carter should have earned some trust and respect by now.

But Carter was still an outsider, never mind he'd lived in Riverbend since he was thirteen, never mind Olivia Campbell had adopted him. Carter had gotten himself into bad trouble throughout high school, and no one could forget that either. Carter hadn't got his head figured out until Faith came along when he'd been eighteen. He'd cleaned up real quick after that.

Grant remembered walking in on Carter in the nursery they'd set up for Faith. Carter, scared shitless that he had this little baby to take care of, had been looking into the crib in silent wonder. His hand had lowered to touch Faith's downy hair, his big fingers shaking.

He'd pulled back when Grant came in, then Carter's terrified look had gone defiant. "I'm gonna take care of her," he'd said, balling one fist. "I don't care what everyone says. I'm gonna take care of her, and I'm not gonna let anyone hurt her. Not ever."

Grant had believed him. From then on, Carter had looked after Faith with fierce intensity.

Even so, it had taken a long time for folks in Riverbend to accept Carter as one of their own, and some were still wary. *We don't know anything about his people,* was the common explanation.

While Kyle had always seemed cool with Carter, Grant guessed that the easygoing acceptance stopped when it came to Carter dating Kyle's sister.

Screw that. If Grace Malory had the hots for Carter, it was none of Kyle's business. If she could draw Carter out of himself and make him happy, so much the better.

Grant would have to see what he could do about that.

"Thanks, Carter," Grant said. He slid on the coat, which hung the tiniest bit loose—Carter was slightly broader in the chest. "Kiss Faith good night for me, all right?"

His mood better, he made for the tent, determined to talk to Christina.

His good mood evaporated, though, when he saw Christina leaving out the other side of the tent with Ray Malory, their arms around each other.

***

Ray was very drunk, barely able to walk as they stumbled up the hill to the vehicles outside the house. Christina had already taken away his keys, and now she shoved him into the passenger side of her pickup, shut the door, and came around the driver's side.

"You don't have to take me home." Ray slurred the words out as she got in. "Kyle can do it."

"Kyle wants to stay and have fun. So do your sisters. I'm done. No reason I can't run you back to town."

Christina said her good-byes to Bailey as soon as she'd thrown her bouquet—which Lucy Malory caught—and Christina had been looking for an excuse to leave. She didn't like that Grant had disappeared in the darkness with the woman Carter had brought to meet him, but she wasn't certain she wanted to face Grant again either.

Ray scowled, dark brows drawing down over bloodshot green eyes. "If you're doing this to make Grant jealous ..."

"Grant has nothing to do with it." Christina shoved her key into the ignition and cranked the truck to life. "He has nothing to do with my life anymore, all right?"

Ray growled something but subsided. Christina knew the lie for what it was—she was leaving to avoid Grant—but the second part of her statement was true. She and Grant were finished, didn't matter that they'd thrown themselves at each other tonight under the trees.

Thrown themselves together, then grabbed hold, kissing, touching, needing. Christina shivered at the remembered sensation of Grant's hand hard between her legs, his fingers coaxing pleasure from her.

Christina hadn't been touched like that in a long time. She'd been to bed with Ray more than a few times, but it was different. Ray was not a bad lover, by any means, but what she'd had with Grant ...

Had been unsettling. So potent she wasn't sure she could handle it again.

Not that she was likely to get the chance. She and Grant had found themselves in an unusual situation, both of them hyped up from the wedding. Christina couldn't blame what she'd done on drink—she had been sipping ginger ale instead of champagne. She couldn't speak for Grant.

No, their bodies had simply reacted to being close to each other's, and they'd not stopped themselves.

It was what it was, Christina told herself. *Move on.*

Ray was very quiet as she drove the five miles into town. He nodded off against the window, his hands relaxed on his thighs. A relief, because Christina didn't want to talk.

The ranch where Ray lived with Kyle and Grace was on the road that led out the north side of town, which entailed driving around the town square. The county courthouse sat in the middle of the square amid a green lawn. The sheriff's department, where Ross worked, was here too.

Shops lined the streets around the square, from souvenir places for the Hill Country tourists, to an old bookstore, to a hardware store, to lawyers' offices, to the feed store at the end. The corner on the northwest side held Mrs. Ward's restaurant and the gas station.

The hardware store had once been a drugstore, complete with an old-fashioned soda fountain. Christina's grandmother had shopped there as a kid, meeting her grandfather for a malted at the soda counter. Christina liked to picture them there, even though the sign over the store said *Hal's Hardware* now.

Ray drawled next to her, "Too bad it's all going to go."

Christina jumped. She hadn't realized he'd woken up. "Go? What's going to go?"

"This." Ray waved an unsteady hand at the slowly passing buildings. "Some developer is trying to buy up the whole town. To make it one big suburb with rows of identical houses and a shopping center."

"Seriously?" Christina ground to a halt at the stop sign next to the feed store, even though no one else was around. "Where'd you hear that?"

"Mrs. Ward told me." Ray settled his head back on the seat. "Yesterday, I think. They made her an offer on her restaurant. She said no, and they were seriously p.o.'d. She said they acted like she was a dumb hick for turning it down. Dickheads."

Christina stared at him for a moment or two before she pulled away from the stop sign and drove on toward the highway. She hadn't heard anything about offers for Mrs. Ward's store, but she'd been focused on the wedding, and on avoiding Grant.

Interesting. She'd have to ask her uncle, Sam Farrell, who owned the bar. Sam knew everything going on in town that was worth knowing.

The Malory ranch was on a fairly flat piece of land north of town. The house had been there for about a hundred years, the Malory family about fifty.

A barn lay beyond the house, surrounded by huge fenced pastures. While Kyle and Ray were most known for their bull-riding skills, they also trained cutting horses for both the rodeo circuit and for cattle work on the big ranches.

The house was dark with Kyle, Grace, and Lucy still at the reception. Ray had gone back to sleep by the time Christina parked in the driveway, and she had to dig into Ray's pants' pocket for his keys.

She took him in through the back—only company used the front door. Ray was hanging on her, half awake and stumbling as Christina got him up the stairs of the two-story house.

Christina knew which one was Ray's bedroom, and she took him there now, arranging him on one side of his big bed.

He was out. Christina put her hands on her hips, studying him.

Ray was a big man, strong, but right now he was completely limp, one arm hanging over the side of the bed. He hadn't been part of the wedding party, so he was in a regular suit, the coat bunched up his back.

Christina sighed. She wouldn't feel right leaving him alone like this. She still cared about Ray — they'd always been friends. She'd stay to make sure he was okay, at least until Kyle or the girls got home.

She pulled off Ray's boots, loosened and slid off his tie, and eased his coat from him, then his pants. She pulled a blanket over his bare legs, folded the clothes neatly on the dresser, and looked at him again.

Ray snored softly, his mouth slack, dark hair rumpled. He really was handsome, even sound asleep.

Standing in the darkened room, Christina made the decision to let him go. It gave her pain to do it, because she'd never know if she and Ray could have had something together.

But it wasn't fair to Ray that Christina's breath left her every time Grant walked into a room, that she was aware of every move Grant made even when she didn't look at him, that she felt sad whenever he walked out again.

Ray deserved to be with a woman who was entirely into *him*. He deserved to fall madly in love, get married, and have half a dozen kids. The kids would love horses like he did, and maybe grow up to be champion bull riders.

Christina would tell him tomorrow, once he got over his hangover, that their current coolness wasn't a temporary fight. They could never be together, not while Grant was there in her heart.

She sighed again. She was tired, she needed to rest, and there was no chair in Ray's bedroom. Plenty of room on the bed, though. Two days ago, she would have climbed up without a second thought. Now, though ... She'd step across the hall to Grace's room, and then go home when Kyle or the sisters turned up.

Ray moaned in his sleep. He was drunker than usual, and she wondered if he'd imbibed more because of his anger at her. Another moan, then the poor guy started to get sick.

Christina hurried into the bathroom, grabbed a towel, and managed to get his head over the edge of the bed, the towel to his mouth. He retched up some spit, then settled down again. Christina folded the towel over and put it into the laundry chute in the hall, then went back to the bedroom.

She worried about leaving him alone in here, even as close as Grace's room was. If he choked...

She could at least take care of him one last night.

Christina wouldn't be able to lie down comfortably in the gown. She reached around to unzip it, then slipped it off, stepping out of her high heels. Christina wrapped a blanket around her body and lay down in her underwear on the empty side of the bed. She'd lie there until someone came home, then hand off Ray's care to them.

As soon as Christina closed her eyes, though, she drifted off. She went to a place of dreams where Grant Campbell smiled at her, his tux coat and shirt sliding from his body as he plied her with his wicked touch.

***

Christina swam awake to find a large arm pinning her to an equally large body. Ray nuzzled her neck.

"Morning, sweetheart," he said in his slow drawl. "If I have to wake up feeling like this, at least I have something beautiful to look at."

Chapter Six

Christina scrambled away from Ray and out of the bed.

It was broad daylight, sunshine pouring through Ray's windows. She smelled coffee brewing below and the sharp scent of bacon.

Crap, crap, crap. Christina snatched up her dress, struggling to slide it on.

"Why're you in such a hurry?" Ray couldn't be feeling good, but he sure looked good, sprawled out half-dressed on the bed, his green eyes heavy.

"Because I have to go," Christina babbled. "Things to do. I didn't mean to fall asleep."

"What things?" Ray's affable look faded. "Do you have to do them at the crack of dawn?"

"I have to get home before people see me coming back like this and know I spent the night out here. Everyone saw me leave the reception with you."

"Yeah, and they know we've been going out for a while now, and we sleep together. It's not a big secret."

"I know. It's just …" Christina trailed off, turning in a circle as the zipper in back stuck, her fingers losing hold of the tiny tab.

Ray came off the bed, moving fast for a man with a hangover. He turned Christina around, took hold of the zipper and smoothly drew it up.

"Thanks," Christina said breathlessly.

"Stay for breakfast," Ray said. It wasn't a suggestion.

"I can't. Sorry."

He caught her shoulders as she faced him again. "Why not? It's breakfast. My sisters will be hurt if you run off without tasting it."

"Ray." Christina stopped. Her heart beat rapidly, and she felt like shit. "Why are you forcing me to be mean to you?"

Ray released her. "Because I don't like to be lied to. You obviously weren't happy waking up beside me, and that's never happened before. Are you trying to run back to Grant? Is that it?"

"No." Christina passed a hand through her tumbling hair. "You saw Grant with those girls at the bar. You got mad at me for looking at him; told me to call you when I was over it. Now I realize I'm going to need more time to get my head on straight. I can't ask you to wait while I do that. You have a life."

While she talked, Ray shrugged off his shirt and tossed it on top of the clothes she'd left on his dresser. He stood in a tight undershirt and boxers, muscles stretching the T-shirt across a hard frame.

He looked like a pin-up guy that women would post on social media and drool over. They'd think Christina nuts for dumping him.

Ray folded his arms, which made him more heart-stoppingly handsome than ever. "So, what, you're breaking up with me?"

"I didn't want to do it like this," Christina said in a tired voice. "I wanted to wait until you felt better."

"No, this is good." His voice was a growl, but the words were calm. "Better than you taking me out to a restaurant and giving me a last meal. I'd rather get over the hangover and you walking out at the same time. My big-ass headache might just blot it all out."

"Ray, I'm really sorry," Christina said, her chest aching. "I never meant for you to be hurt—believe me on that. How about if I tell everyone *you* broke up with *me*? I don't want people feeling sorry for you."

"Huh. Don't worry about me, sugar. I won't be crying into my beer over you. I always knew you didn't want anyone but Grant. I just thought we could have some fun, that's all."

Christina's eyes stung. "We did. *I* had fun. I'm so, so sorry."

Ray scowled. "Stop saying you're sorry and take your ass out of here. Especially before you can say, *I hope we'll still be friends.* I haven't decided whether I want to stay friends with you or not. I'm going to be pissed off for a while, all right? Just leave me alone when you see me. If I start being cordial to you, that means maybe I'm ready to be friends again."

"Yeah, all right." Christina rubbed her arms. "I'm so—"

Ray held up his hand. "Crap on a crutch, sweetheart, quit with the *I'm sorry*. It's getting on my nerves. Just leave."

"Okay." Christina tried a smile. "See ya, Ray."

"Sure. See you round."

Christina plucked her handbag from the dresser and hurried out, wincing when Ray slammed the door behind her.

Downstairs, she tried to sneak out the door, but Grace came out of the kitchen and caught her. "Christina? Where you running off to? Lucy and I cooked a big spread—okay, I did the cooking, and Lucy did important things like opening jars."

"Hey," Lucy said, coming out behind Grace. "Opening jars *is* important."

They stood next to each other, Lucy three years older than Grace, the sisters much alike in looks—dark hair, the Malory green eyes. Grace wore her long hair in a ponytail, loved to cook, and had an apron to go with every outfit. Lucy had her hair cut into a businesslike do, and her clothes and makeup were always crisp and neat. In school, Grace had loved home economics and English; Lucy had loved math and business classes.

Grace noticed Christina's moist eyes, and softened her tone. "Christina, what happened? Was my brother a crabby shit to you?"

"No ... not his fault." Christina shook her head. "Why didn't you wake me up? I didn't mean to stay the rest of the night."

"Because when I peeked in, you were sleeping like a baby, and I thought ..." Grace spread her hands.

Lucy finished, "She thought you and Ray had been getting busy. No?"

"No," Christina said. She let out a breath. "Just a warning. We split up, so Ray might be in a bad mood when he comes down. You might not want to mention me at all."

Instead of looking worried, the two girls deflated in disappointment. "Aw, damn," Lucy said. "I was hoping you'd get to be my sister one day."

Christina would have liked that. Another twist to the pain in her heart.

Grace gave her a shrewd look. "Is this because of Grant?" she asked. "I don't want to upset you, but I have to tell you, Christina—last night I saw him walking a woman out to her car. When he came back, he was disheveled, if you know what I mean, mud all over his coat. I hate to say it, but you need to know. I don't like to see you breaking your heart on him."

Lucy nodded in support.

Christina suspected that the woman in question had been the one she'd seen Carter with when he'd come looking for Grant. Christina had stayed long enough to watch the woman hand Grant a business card, and the three of them start chatting. Someone who wanted to hire them, no doubt. Carter had probably asked Grant to see her to her car.

Grant had been rumpled because he'd been having a grope session with Christina, not the mystery woman. Christina decided not to enlighten Lucy and Grace about that.

Christina gave them each a hug and a kiss. "You two are terrific friends. Thanks for the breakfast invitation, but I don't think I should stay. I don't want to upset Ray any more than I already have, and I just need to be by myself for a while."

Grace and Lucy said they understood, though they remained disappointed.

Christina finally got out of there and into her car, her tulle bow now a tired lump.

She drove back into town, the road blurry from her tears. When she pulled up at the stop sign at the square, it was to see Grant and one of the guys who worked at the Campbells' ranch getting out of Grant's truck outside the feed store.

Grant, not three feet from her, glanced over, and stilled. He took in Christina's mussed hair and her wrinkled bridesmaid's dress, and his mouth went hard.

He turned away without acknowledging her, walking with his guy around the feed store to where bales of hay were stacked behind it.

Christina had a good view of Grant's fine ass in tight jeans, but it was the back of him saying good-bye. Maybe even *good riddance*.

***

Doing a stunt with a train was always dangerous. Grant set up a meeting with the train restoration society, and the following Friday took Tyler with him to go look at the site.

The club had been founded in the last year, and recently, they'd bought a piece of track about forty miles west of Riverbend, on a line no longer used. The area was flat, with grasslands drier than those of River County. Grant had known about the place but never had cause to go there before now. Grant liked the look of it when he arrived—level ground was better for stunt work.

Karen made sure the engineer was expecting them. The restored steam engine was a thing of beauty, as fully functional as it had been a hundred and forty years ago. It pulled a train of three passenger cars and a baggage car, also well restored.

This particular engine and cars had been used in movies and TV before, and the engineer who'd bought it and moved here from California was familiar with setting up shots. He invited them for a ride, and they went around the mile-long circle of track.

Halfway along, Grant had the engineer slow the train, and he and Tyler got out to observe it move from the ground.

When the train circled back around to them, first Grant, then Tyler, ran and jumped up onto the cars. Decent hand and foot holds, Grant found, and the driver knew how to keep the train running at an even pace.

Grant and Tyler let themselves into the passenger cars and walked their length inside. The train had been restored with polished wood, velvet seats, and gleaming windows with tasseled shades. It even had a restored metal water jug with spigot for thirsty passengers.

The brothers went out onto the back platform and climbed to the top of the car. The train was going at snail speed, but everything swayed a lot.

They sat down on the roof, enjoying the panorama of the wide Texas land under a huge sky as the train took them back toward the depot.

"So Karen Marvin," Tyler said. Karen had come to the ranch a couple times this week, to go through paperwork with Carter. "You know, she's not bad looking—in a tight-assed businesswoman kind of way. But hey, when the suit comes off, and the hair comes out of the bun, those ladies are all woman, just like any other."

Grant hid a grin. "Ask her out then."

"Can't while I'm going out with Jeannette. Even I need to do things one at a time, bro."

Grant went through Tyler's conquests but couldn't place this one. Must be recent. "Who's Jeannette?"

"You met her at Adam's party, remember?"

Grant's memory cleared. "Oh, *that* Jeannette. The stripper."

"Exotic dancer," Tyler corrected him. "We got to talking, and hit it off." He shrugged.

Of course they had. Tyler's libido was legendary.

Tyler frowned at him. "Take that disapproving look off your face, all right? There's nothing wrong with her."

Grant lifted his hands. "Did I say anything? Just be careful."

"I think *you* need to watch yourself. I saw Karen looking at you like she wanted to grab you and start chewing on you." Tyler looked down as they approached the depot. "And speak of the devil."

Karen was waiting on the small platform with Carter and another man from the historical society. She tilted her head back, saw Tyler and Grant sitting on top of the car, and waved. She was in a dark blue skirted business suit today, had her hair in a swept-back French braid, and wore sunglasses against the glare.

Grant caught the bars of the ladder, descended a few rungs, then jumped the rest of the way to the platform.

"Looks okay," Grant said to Carter, who waited for his report. "Solid—nothing's going to fall apart on us. Good handholds, plus they'll let us put on others if we need them."

Karen had taken off her sunglasses and nibbled one of the earpieces as Grant spoke.

"I think we can do this," Tyler added. "Train cars are good and sturdy."

"Great," Karen said. "Then we can get started right away. How about if I take you boys to lunch, and we can discuss the script?"

Tyler tipped his hat and gave her a polite smile. "No can do, ma'am, but thanks. I have a ton of stuff going on at the ranch I gotta get back to. Nice meeting you again." He did the hat thing one more time, then settled it on his head, winked at Karen, and walked out through the depot.

"Then it's us three?" Karen asked.

Carter shook his head. "I have another meeting. Grant will go over the script with you and talk about what needs to be done. He's good at that."

Grant felt a burning in his chest, but he put on a smile. "Sure, be happy to."

They walked through the small depot, thanking the guys in the historical society once more. Grant dropped a twenty into their fund-raising jar, then followed Karen and Carter out.

Carter said good-bye and headed for his truck. Karen started toward the BMW she'd driven the night of the wedding. Grant had ridden out here with Tyler, who was already gone, so his choices of transportation were drying up fast.

"Hang on a sec, ma'am," Grant said to Karen. "Just got to remind my brother of something."

Karen nodded, unworried, and unlocked her car. Grant quickened his stride to catch up with Carter.

"What the hell are you doing, throwing me to the wolves?" Grant asked him.

Carter turned around, his hazel eyes cool. "I really do have another meeting. I know she's a man-eater, but suck it up. Don't blow this deal, Grant. We need the money."

Grant let out his breath. He was used to women chasing after him, but the buckle bunnies were usually starry-eyed and a little sweet, even the most determined ones. Predatory women were not his thing.

He gave Carter a curt nod. "All right, I got this. But you owe me."

"Sure." Carter was done with the conversation. He pointedly got into his truck and slammed the door.

Karen was already in the car by the time Grant reached it. She smiled at him when he got in and tugged on his seatbelt.

The sedan was cushy, top of the line, with leather seats that cradled Grant's butt, individual climate control for each passenger, and a state-of-the-art sound system, the whole works. The doors locked with a loud click, a sound Grant didn't like.

"Let's go to that cute restaurant you have in Riverbend," Karen said. "I've been dying to try it. Real down-home food, right? Tell me it's not so down-home that it's all roaches and rats and chicken-fried steak."

"Mrs. Ward keeps her place clean," Grant said. "We have health inspectors even out here. But she does make a mean chicken-fried steak."

"I'll have to be guided by you on my menu choices then."

Grant knew damn well that if he walked into Ward's Family Restaurant with this woman on his arm, it would be all over town by mid-afternoon.

But what the hell? He hadn't heard from Christina all week, hadn't seen her since she'd pulled up outside the feed store the morning after the wedding. He'd been there because a whole pile of hay bales at the ranch had spoiled. Grant had called the owner, asking the man to open up for him, even if it was a Sunday.

He'd heard a car stop, and there had been Christina, just woken up and still in her wedding clothes. Something sour had bit his stomach, and he'd turned away, unable to look anymore.

He knew from Grace Malory that Christina had moved out of her apartment and into Bailey's house, now that Bailey would be living with Adam, but that's all Grant knew. Grant had kept away from town, staying at Circle C and working until he drove home and fell into bed. He didn't want to go to the bar and see Christina, so Grant's social life had narrowed to his family.

If the good folks of Riverbend wanted to think Grant Campbell had become the boy toy of a rich city woman, let them.

"All right," he said, trying to sound enthusiastic. "You bet."

Chapter Seven

As Grant led Karen into the restaurant, he felt a distinct chill around him. People glanced up, watched him go by, eyes stony.

Their looks weren't knowing or amused. These were the hostile gazes of unhappy people.

Oh, come on. Everyone already knew about the Campbells starting a new stunt riding project, and how Karen had come out from Houston, staying in Fredericksburg while she watched the shoot. The woman had come to the wedding reception, for crying out loud. Grant hadn't noticed hostile looks then.

They couldn't be mad at him for Christina's sake, either. The whole town had watched Grant and Christina date other people since their breakup, and they'd already picked a side.

So what was going on?

Grant ushered Karen into an empty booth and took the seat opposite her. Karen, oblivious of the scrutiny, took the menu from its slot on the table and opened it.

"This place is so cute," she said, glancing around at the potted plants, the white curtains, the photos on the walls of Riverbend through the years. She liked that word — *cute*. "I can see why you all come here."

"It's also the only place in town." Grant had taken off his hat upon entering, and now he dropped it onto the seat beside him. "Mrs. Ward is one hell of a cook. People from one of those food channel shows came out here to meet her, and challenged her to a cook-off. Mrs. Ward won."

Karen gave a laugh with her neatly lipsticked mouth. "Mrs. Ward doesn't have a first name?"

Grant shrugged. "Sure, but she's a pillar of Riverbend. Her family's lived here for decades. It's a sign of respect, calling her Mrs. Ward."

"Your family has lived here for decades," Karen pointed out. "Your mom told me to call her Olivia."

Grant folded his arms across the menu, trying to hang on to his patience. "My mom is different. She had to raise five kids on her own. Five boys. Made her tough."

"So *she* gets a first name and Mrs. Ward doesn't?"

"Mrs. Ward likes to be called Mrs. Ward," Grant said, a bit stiffly. "It's the way it is."

"Don't get mad, sweetie. I'm only trying to understand." She glanced around. "Any way we can get some water? And order? I love getting to know you, honey, but I do have a full afternoon."

The waitresses and busboys seemed to be avoiding the table. Grant signaled to a waitress he'd known since he was five, giving her a wave. She disappeared into the kitchen and didn't come out.

Karen was busily texting someone, her thumbs moving, the phone clicking. Maybe that was why everyone in here was annoyed. They didn't like people who couldn't look up from their cell phones to pass the time of day.

Mrs. Ward herself came out of the kitchen and stopped next to the table. "Afternoon, Grant," she said. "What can I get you and your friend?"

She was polite. Too polite. Whatever the hell was going on, the whole restaurant was in on it. "Chicken-fried steak," Grant said. "Mashed potato with mine. What kind of potatoes you want, Ms. Marvin? The twice baked is damn good."

"Whatever you're having is fine with me." Karen glanced up from her phone, gave Mrs. Ward a tight smile, and went back to texting. *Click, click, click.*

Grant sent Mrs. Ward an apologetic look. Mrs. Ward acknowledged this with a nod and marched away. He looked after her, puzzled. Something was seriously wrong when Mrs. Ward was rude.

Karen finally tucked the phone into her purse. "Remember when you told me to call you *Grant*? Well call me Karen. I'm not a venerable pillar of Riverbend ... yet. Have a long way to go before that happens."

"Yeah, okay," Grant said sliding the menus back into their slots. "What about this script?" The only way he could shut out the others watching them was to be all business. Maybe the townsfolk would go back to minding their own.

As Karen pulled the script from her briefcase, two more customers walked in—Christina with Lucy Malory, who apparently hadn't gone back to Houston yet.

Great.

Christina looked across the restaurant. Her eyes flickered when she saw Grant.

Just like that, Grant was transported to the darkness under the trees the night of Adam's wedding, Christina's breath on his lips, her touch firm on his cock. Her curves had been supple under his hands, and the heat between her legs had told him she was as greedy for him as he'd been for her.

Christina's look cooled, and she turned away as she and Lucy sought a table. The only one open was behind Grant on the other side of the restaurant. He could see the two women in the mirror behind Karen, if he bent his head a little.

" … And then after a hard day's train robbing, shooting, and fighting," Karen said, "you and your fellow bandits ride up to your ranch house and realize you have to do your laundry. Robbing a train is dirty work. The only thing that gets the stains out is our client's detergent."

Grant dragged his attention back to the pages Karen was showing him. "Yeah, that's real funny," he said.

"We'll tweak it to whatever you recommend, as long as the message gets across. A seriously entertaining commercial gets people to remember a product."

Grant couldn't argue with that. His favorite commercials of all time were for a brand of beer he couldn't stand.

The chicken-fried steak took a long time to come out—people were finishing lunch and leaving—but Karen didn't seem to mind. Her full schedule must not worry her, or else she was willing to make people wait.

When the food finally arrived, plunked down by an unsmiling Mrs. Ward, Grant was afraid she'd have made the steaks tasteless to show her disapproval of Karen.

The first bite put his fears to rest. Mrs. Ward took a lot of pride in her cooking; she'd never make a bad meal.

"This is good," Karen said, as though she'd expected otherwise. "Can't be good for you, though. Everything on this plate is white."

"People have been eating white food for centuries," Grant said. "And we're all still here."

"True," Karen conceded. She took another tiny bite. "You have a good way of putting things, Grant. I like that."

Grant wasn't certain he liked her liking it. He tried to enjoy his lunch, but it was tough with Christina's eyes on the back of his head. He knew she was watching him, because whenever he looked into the mirror, her gaze was on him.

Christina was beautiful today, her short black hair curling every which way, a tank top with skinny straps showing off her hot body. Grant was going to get a kink in his neck staring at her.

Her coffee-dark eyes were fixed on Grant, which was about the only thing Grant remembered about that lunch with Karen Marvin. The chicken-fried steak, the script, Karen's smooth voice, the cold stares of the townspeople … none of it mattered.

All that mattered was Christina looking at him, and the hunger in his heart.

***

Christina needed to warn him. She realized Grant
had no idea what was wrong as he sat talking to the
ice-queen from hell. His smiles had been too
forthcoming, his laugh too easy.

He didn't know the entire town was furious at
Karen Marvin. The way he nodded at everyone as he
rose from the booth and walked Karen out told her
that. He was the usual charming Grant, everyone's
friend.

Christina watched him settle his black cowboy hat
on his head as he ushered Karen from the restaurant.
His hand hovered at the small of Karen's back as he
walked her into the street and opened the driver's
side door of her car for her. Grant then walked
around the car to the passenger side and got in with
her.

As soon as his door closed, the diner exploded in
gossip, heavy with disapproval. *Did you see that? Can
you believe a Campbell would do such a thing? Why is
Grant with her?*

"He doesn't know," Christina said loudly, angry
on his behalf. The sleek BMW started up and pulled
smoothly away from the curb, a chance reflection
flashing into the restaurant. "No one told him."

"Oh, come on," a guy from the feed store said.
"Everyone knows."

"He was being polite to her," Mrs. Ward put in.
"She was his guest, a business client, and he couldn't
make a scene. Just shows his good upbringing." She
glared pointedly at the man who'd spoken.

Christina knew Grant better than anyone, and one
thing Grant Campbell was not was *subtle*. If Grant
had an opinion on something, everyone on the
planet knew. If he'd been angry at Karen, his

politeness would have been tinged with chill, not friendliness.

Christina fished out money for her sandwich and drink, and squirmed out from the booth. "I'm going to go talk to him," she told Lucy.

Lucy looked as though she hadn't decided who to believe, but she nodded. "Do what you gotta. I have a lot of packing to finish." Lucy was heading back to Houston tomorrow, her visit home over.

Christina squeezed her hand. "See you before you go."

Lucy squeezed her hand in return, but she didn't try to make Christina linger. She understood Christina's hurry.

"Disgrace to his mama," an older man muttered as Christina went by him. "I told Olivia he was no good after he drove his pickup right into my store."

Grant had been fifteen. He'd worked all through high school to pay for the damage, Christina remembered. Grant and Adam had been wild boys, but they'd always righted their wrongs.

Christina left the diner, jumped into her truck, and drove away from the biggest gossips in Riverbend.

She was getting tired of living in a fishbowl. When she'd gone to stay with Lucy in Houston for a week this January, she'd been amazed at the anonymity of the city.

Lucy had told her that there were pockets of neighborhoods where people were close, but what Christina saw were folks so busy with their own lives they didn't have time to worry about hers. Walking around shopping without the entire town knowing exactly what she'd bought, for whom, and why, had been refreshing.

Christina had never minded Riverbend's propensity to talk about everyone and everything when she'd been younger. It hadn't bothered her until she and Grant had broken up.

Then, suddenly, everyone in the county had to weigh in. Christina had made the right choice, some said. Others said Christina was a heartless bitch who should have stuck with Grant no matter what.

They speculated that she and Grant couldn't have kids because Christina worked at a bar, and Grant drank too much. Others said that, in truth, they weren't sleeping together all. Or, God was punishing them for living in sin. Didn't matter that they were at church together almost every Sunday.

Some said that Christina and Grant had such kinky sex there was no way babies could come of it. Another opinion was that Christina had used too much birth control as a teenager, because she was a tramp, and now she was paying for it.

On and on, whether sympathetic or unkind, opinions on Christina's personal life had sailed around her. Most had been wildly off the mark, but others were too close to what she feared, like using birth control pills for too long before she and Grant had tried to have a baby. Or maybe she'd waited too long, period. A woman's fertility decreased as she got older.

Christina was sick and tired of it. Maybe this new situation in town would goad her to make the decision to leave, move to Houston and stay with Lucy. Lucy promised that Christina would have a job quickly, and a place of her own soon after that.

Clean slate, start over, with no memories to punch Christina in the face every time she turned a corner.

She arrived at Grant's trailer, pulling her truck around the back so it wouldn't be visible from the road. Hers was the only vehicle around, telling her that Grant and Karen had probably returned to the Campbell ranch for business. She tried to call him, but Grant didn't answer his cell phone.

He rarely did. Grant wasn't a cell phone kind of guy. He'd put the phone down somewhere and forget about it, or he'd keep it muted and not bother to check messages.

He didn't text either, saying his thumbs were too big for it. Carter and Tyler did all the talking on the business phone while Grant kept things face-to-face and friendly.

Christina knew she could have gone to the ranch and waited to talk to him, but Grant's family would be there. Olivia would want to be polite and sit with Christina, offering her iced tea and snacks, which would only add soreness to her heart. Plus, she couldn't warn Grant about Karen if he was with Karen.

Christina knew deep down why she'd made these excuses to herself and driven to his house. She wanted to see him alone. Wanted to so much, she was willing to wait for him to finish for the afternoon and return home.

It was hot today, especially for March. Christina would soon bake in the truck, so she got out and climbed the step to Grant's front door. It was unlocked—Grant never locked his doors.

Grant had bought the trailer after he and Christina had broken up, and she'd never seen its interior. She'd driven past it plenty of times, of course, and had been unable to stop herself glancing at it, swallowing hard if she saw his truck parked in front.

Seeing the leather reclining chair set in front of the television almost broke her heart. He'd bought it from a friend right after they'd moved in together, and she'd complained about how worn out it already was. But Grant had insisted it was perfect, and Christina admitted it was comfortable as hell.

She and Grant had made love in that chair.

She quickly turned away. A new sofa sat along the front wall, along with a new coffee table, but Christina's gaze kept catching memories.

Pictures of Grant's family. Photos of Grant on horseback, in costume, usually as a Wild West bandit. With Tyler, arms folded and looking mean in their black hats, fake handlebar mustaches, and black shirts. Another photo showed him and his four brothers in T-shirts and jeans, all laughing at the camera.

A photo sitting in the middle of the cluster made her stop, her heart squeezing. It was a picture of her and Grant, smiling and happy. She remembered when that picture had been taken—at a picnic out by the river. Tyler had snapped the photo of Grant with his arms around Christina from behind, his face next to hers, Grant looking at the camera as though daring the viewer to guess what they were going to do later.

She set down the picture, her heart heavy.

Christina knew Grant had hired a cleaning team to come in after the bachelor party, but already the trailer wasn't pristine. Grant dropped clothes as he took them off, to lie there until laundry day. Dishes from breakfast rested in the sink and on the small counter.

Christina started to pick up his clothes. She tried to make herself stop—she didn't live with him anymore—but she couldn't help it. She smoothed the black T-shirt and worn jeans over her arm and carried them to the hamper in the bathroom. Then she went out and started rinsing off the dishes.

As she worked, every single thing she'd tried to shut out for the last year and more came back to her.

Grant leaning on the kitchen counter as she worked, a towel in his big hands, not too macho to help out with the dishes. Grant kissing her when the chores were done, smiling as he backed her to the chair. They'd settle on it, Christina on his lap as they watched TV, talked, or kissed. Then they'd go to the bedroom for spread-out, enthusiastic sex. Laughing and talking, or arguing and making up, until they fell asleep.

They'd wake in the morning, in the sunshine, wrapped in each other. Grant would rumble that he had to go to work and Christina would stay in bed, soaking in the warmth he left.

After they'd broken up, Christina had deliberately pushed every memory of him aside, knowing she couldn't handle them.

As she stood now in the middle of Grant's living room, the memories hurtled at her with the speed of a summer storm and she was defenseless.

Tears welled up and spilled from her eyes. When everything had gone wrong between them, it had hurt with gut-ripping pain. The only way to stop the pain had been to walk away.

The pain hadn't stopped, though, Christina realized in dismay. She'd simply pretended it didn't exist.

But all the old pain and sorrows were here, in this room. She could hear their wall-shaking arguments, the things they'd said that cut, and again their laughter, and their cries of passion as they relieved their unstoppable need for each other.

She shouldn't have come. Christina took a breath and headed for the door. She'd explain the situation to Olivia, have her talk to Grant.

As she reached the door, she saw Karen Marvin's BMW pull up in the drive and stop. The engine switched off. Grant emerged from the passenger side, strolled around, and opened the door for Karen.

The two of them headed for the house.

Christina panicked, ran for Grant's bedroom, and hid in the closet.

Chapter Eight

"Well, this is cute," Christina heard Karen say.

Grant's laughter rumbled. "That's one word for it. It's a trailer in the middle of nowhere. Not much, but it's home for now."

"I like it," Karen said.

The door clicked closed and the floor creaked. "Want coffee? Or iced tea? We should have gone to the ranch — all kinds of good stuff up there."

"No, I wanted to speak to you alone."

"About the script?" Grant's voice held skepticism. For all his courtesy, Christina reflected, Grant wasn't stupid.

"About the deal. I'd rather negotiate with you. Your brother Carter is a good businessman, but he's a little unnerving."

"He's fine," Grant said with a growl. Christina liked that Grant always jumped to Carter's defense, had even when they'd been kids and Carter had just beaten the shit out of him. "He's not good at talking, but he's okay. Now, Tyler and me, we don't know when to shut up."

"Carter isn't from Riverbend, is he?" Karen sounded interested. "He doesn't act like the rest of you. He was adopted?"

"It's no secret." Grant clattered cups, ran water. "He was sent to our ranch as part of a rehab thing. My mom was in a program to help kids like him learn how to take care of horses and ride. My mom liked Carter and decided to adopt him."

Christina knew that there had been much more to it than that, but Grant didn't like to go into it with outsiders.

"How sweet," Karen said. "Now, let's you and I *talk*."

There was a thump, a rattle, and then Grant said, "Whoa."

The sounds became muffled, Karen laughing, Grant's replies inaudible.

Christina couldn't stand it. Plastered against the wall of Grant's closet, she could see nothing, no longer hear. She crept out, making no noise, until she peeked through the half-opened bedroom door.

She had a view of the kitchen, of Grant backed hard against the counter. Karen snatched her hands out of Grant's grasp to start unbuttoning his shirt.

"Don't worry, honey," Karen said. "You've got this deal set in stone. What we do or don't do today won't change that. But you're a big, hot cowboy, and I need me some of that."

Grant caught her wrists again. "Not the time or place."

"I disagree. This is *exactly* the time and place." Karen was all smiles, a determined glint in her eyes.

She got her hands free once more and yanked open Grant's shirt. Buttons pinged onto the floor and counter, and into the sink.

Karen's hands with their long nails went to his bare skin. "I think we can make a side deal here. I scratch *your* chest—you scratch mine."

She took her fingers from Grant long enough to pop open the first three buttons of her own blouse. A bra of hot pink lace came into view.

Christina's heart pounded in sickening beats. She could not stay here if Grant and that woman were going to have sex on the kitchen counter.

But the only way out was past them. The windows in the bedroom were too small to crawl though. No way was she going try, maybe get stuck, maybe fall on her face to the ground. She was well and truly screwed.

Grant caught Karen's hands one more time. "Sorry, sweetheart. I can't."

"Why? You married?"

"No …"

"Girlfriend? Is this her?" Karen swung away to snatch up the photo of Grant and Christina in better days. "I saw her watching you at the diner."

"Yeah." Grant grabbed the picture from her and put it carefully back on the shelf.

"You're not together anymore, though, are you?" Karen asked. "I heard you broke up. If you were still together, she'd have been all up in your shit for being with another woman."

"Doesn't matter," Grant said. "I'm not for sale."

"I told you, this isn't part of the deal. You're just beautiful." Karen slid her hands inside Grant's open shirt. "I love a man with chest hair. So sexy. Where does this go?" She traced Grant's glory trail to his waistband and tried to pop open his belt buckle.

Grant trapped her wrists again. "Look, sweetie, you're real nice, but not right now. I got a million things to do up at the ranch, and—"

Karen broke free, but heaved a long sigh. "Don't lie, honey. I can take it. You don't want me." She started buttoning her blouse, hiding the bra. "I'm coming on too strong, and you're used to women who are sweet and polite." She batted her lashes and let her voice become high-pitched. "Ooh, Grant, are you interested in little ole me? I never dreamed … not me … poor little wallflower."

Grant didn't bother to respond. He started to do up his shirt, realized she'd busted off the buttons, and gave up.

Karen finished with her blouse and took up her purse. "I'll be patient," she said.

She let her gaze rove over Grant, who leaned back on the counter, hands bracing, shirt open, hair tousled. Christina had to agree—he was beautiful.

"You're worth waiting for. Rowrrr." Karen made a cat-claw gesture then swung around and sauntered out of the trailer, straightening the blouse and suit coat as she went.

Christina heard the chirp of a car door unlocking then the smooth hum of the BMW engine starting up, the crunch of gravel as Karen drove away.

"Shit!" Grant said vehemently.

He picked up a coffee cup, ready to throw it, then slammed the un-drunk coffee into the sink and plunked the cup onto the counter. The second batch of coffee followed, then he ripped the coffee maker's plug out of the wall.

Grant stamped toward the bedroom. Christina retreated as fast as she could, but there was nowhere to go. She was only a few feet from the door when he slapped it open.

A startled yell launched from Grant's mouth when he saw Christina, and he hurtled backward, straight into the door. His head made an audible *crack*.

"Grant." Christina went to him in alarm. "You okay?"

"Son of a bitch! Christina, what the holy hell are you doing here?"

Christina danced between hurt and the absurdity of the situation. She decided to go with absurd.

"Aw," she drawled in imitation of Karen. "Honey, you're just beautiful." She shoved the placket of Grant's shirt aside and pressed her fingers flat to his chest. "You're a big, hot cowboy, and I need me some of that."

"Christina." Grant caught her hands, just as he'd caught Karen's. "What are you doing sneaking into my place?"

Christina didn't answer. She jerked free and ran her fingers down the arrow of hair on his abdomen. "Ooo, where does *this* go?"

"Quit that." Grant's body started to shake with laughter.

Christina slid her hands to his nipples, dark against his bronze-colored skin. "And what are *these*? Do you like that? Oh, I *love* me a man with chest hair."

"Christina ... damn it." Grant grabbed her hands again. "Stop!"

"Oh, you *do* like it." Christina kept her fingers over the tips of his nipples. She was mad and reckless, loving being next to him, and she didn't care.

"Sweetheart …"

"I just want to *eat* you up." Christina leaned close, flicking his nipple with her tongue.

"Baby …"

His word died into a groan as Christina wrapped her lips around the hard point and started to suck.

Grant had always liked her playing with his chest, though he never admitted it out loud. The thought of Karen touching him there, maybe triggering his excitement, pissed Christina off.

Only *she* got to do that. Christina pressed her palm over his zipper and had a flush of satisfaction to find him rising to her hand.

"Now, come on," Grant said, but his voice had gone soft.

Christina popped his belt buckle then opened his jeans. Any fight in him died into breathless silence as she undid the zipper and pushed the jeans and underwear down his hips.

Grant's cock spilled out, thick and hard, caught in Christina's hand. The familiar weight and girth of it brought the five years of her life she'd tried to push away slamming back into her, as though their time apart hadn't existed.

This place, this bedroom, including the bed they'd slept in together, contained so much of *him*. The onslaught of memories, the scent of him, tangled her in bonds that wouldn't let go.

Christina found herself sliding down his body to land on her knees on the soft rug. His jeans sagged, baring his thighs tight with muscle, not an ounce of fat—hard from riding, supple from all the running and acrobatics he did. Between those legs hung a part of him Christina had missed seeing. Grant's cock had dark hair at its base, the rest of it smooth and taut.

Grant curled his fists at his sides as Christina plied him with her tongue, more memories flooding back when she tasted the spice of his skin.

Memories must have come at him too, because he tangled his fingers in her hair, just as he'd done whenever she'd gone down on him in their bedroom … or living room, kitchen, pickup truck, the dense shadows of the rodeo grounds parking lot. "Christina," he said in his low, dark voice.

No more fighting, no more protesting. They were Christina and Grant once again.

Christina slid her mouth over his cock, drawing it all the way inside her.

Grant's hand tightened in her hair. He whispered, "Damn," but didn't stop her. His hips moved, rocking in time to what she did with her mouth.

She licked and suckled, rubbed her tongue on him, nibbled his tip. Grant smoothed her hair, cupped her head, leaned back against the door frame to let her reach all she wanted.

Christina looked up Grant's long, tall body, his shirt hanging open, to the brush of dark whiskers on his face, his closed eyes, his dark hair streaked by sunshine.

I love him so much.

The words scared her. Christina focused again on what she was doing, pulling harder with her mouth.

She planted her hands on his thighs, steadying herself and enjoying his body.

She could tell when he was about to come. He let go of her to ball his fists. His hips rocked faster, and choked groans came from his throat.

Just before Christina thought she'd feel the heat of his seed in her mouth, he put his hands under her arms and jerked her to his feet.

Not to stop her. Grant's eyes were burning blue, his grip closing around her and not letting go.

"No," he said, voice rasping. "Not when you're with someone else."

Christina wet her lips. "I broke up with Ray. For good."

It took a second for that news to register in his brain. Then Grant's eyes went flat. He hauled Christina the few steps to the bed, kicked off his jeans, and nearly ripped her shorts off.

His open shirt brushed her as Grant came over her. His eyes held so much anger, and yet so much need.

Christina was pushed back into the mattress, Grant's weight on her, then he parted her thighs and slid himself inside her. Completing her.

***

Grant had no thoughts, no regrets, just being inside Christina until he couldn't feel anything else.

Nothing but her body closing around him, her lips and tongue, her hands on his back. Karen had pissed him off, and then *damn*, there was Christina.

Between embarrassment, his heart about jumping out of his chest, then Christina going down on him, for fuck's sake, Grant didn't have a chance. Self-control dried up and blew away on the hot Texas wind.

Christina was beautiful, and she was the love of his life. Her dark eyes sparkled, drinking him in, and her arms were around him—where they should be.

He was inside her—she wrapped him and coaxed him, tightening and loosening at just the right moments. They'd learned each other long ago, and their bodies still remembered.

"Damn baby," Grant whispered. "You are *sweet*."

Christina said nothing—she never did. She always loved him silently, fiercely, until the last when her cries of pleasure told him more than words how deep she was feeling what they did.

Grant could never be quiet. He groaned out loud, his hips moving faster, the friction hot, erotic, satisfying.

"And hungry," he said, voice tight. "You are always so hungry, darlin'."

Christina's eyes were half closed, her tongue at her wet lips. Her breasts moved against him, tight nipples brushing his chest. All the while, her hands roved his back, pulling him harder into her.

It was wild, frantic, primal. This was Christina, the only woman Grant had ever loved.

"Aw, fuck," Grant said softly as his release hit him, far sooner than he wanted it to.

Christina rocked against him, desperate, her breath coming fast. Grant slid his hand under him and pressed the tight berry between her legs.

Christina shrieked. Her coming happened then, her body moving in exact time with his, her voice crying his name and making everything all right in his world.

They christened that bed, room, and house then and there, coming together, the two of them one again.

Grant let out a last groan and collapsed onto Christina, gathering the woman he loved to his heart.

***

A long time later, Grant peeled open his eyes. The sun was already heading down, late afternoon light pouring in his west-facing window.

Christina lay on her side against him, one of his arms and his leg around her. Christina was blinking, waking as well.

"Crap," she whispered.

"Shh," Grant said as she tried to pull away. "I don't see anything here to regret." He ran a languid hand through her hair, loving the silky feel of her curls. "Nothing at all."

"I know," Christina said softly. She settled back down, warm against him. "But later, this is going to hurt."

"Why does it have to?" What was *he* talking about? It was hurting already. "Why can't we just enjoy ourselves? Why does it have to be a drama thing?"

"I don't know." Christina slid her hand over his where he cradled her. "It always is, with us."

"Yeah, you got a point." Grant drew his palm across her shoulder. Damn, she was soft. He'd always loved to kiss and lick her satin skin.

"You stopped asking me why I was hiding in your bedroom," Christina said after a silent few moments.

Grant cupped her breast, closing his finger and thumb over her nipple. "I stopped caring."

"I came to warn you about Karen."

Grant really didn't want to talk about Karen. He'd do the commercial, let Carter collect the money, and avoid the woman as much as possible.

Christina went on. "When I saw you in the diner—the way you acted, I could tell you didn't know."

Grant was only marginally interested in town gossip. "Didn't know what?"

Christina turned in his arms to face him. "Karen Marvin runs a development company that wants to buy up every scrap of land in and around Riverbend. They'll bulldoze it, put in housing developments and shopping centers—make it a bedroom community, a suburb called Riverbend Heights. When you brought her to the diner and were so nice to her ... well, everyone jumped to their own conclusions. Most of them think you and your brothers are taking a kickback to help her."

Chapter Nine

Grant stilled, his eyes losing their sexy, languid look. *"Shit."*

Grant's shirt had come off in their frenzy, baring all of him. Christina couldn't help but reach for him, running her hand along his firm shoulder.

"I could tell you didn't know," she said. "You'd never have been so nice to her if you had."

"How do you know this?" Grant demanded. "Why don't *I*?"

"Ray told me," Christina said, flinching a little as she said his name. Not someone she wanted to bring up when she was in Grant's bed. "Mrs. Ward confirmed it, and Ted from the feed store filled in the rest. The company apparently specializes in buying up loans and then finding any way they can to foreclose on the property. They do this all the time, mostly preying on small, older towns, where the land values are depressed. They want Bailey's house — her whole neighborhood — the bar, the diner, all of downtown, and most of the land around it. They'll buy up the small ranches and farms, everything that's privately owned."

"Damn, damn, damn." Grant scrubbed his hand through his hair. "Carter hasn't said a word about that. Does he know?"

Christina had no idea. "I'm only going by what Mrs. Ward and some others told me. So, when they saw you with Karen, the two of you all friendly ..."

"Hell, no wonder everyone looked at me like I'd burned down an orphanage."

"An orphanage with puppies in it," Christina said, then she scowled. "Like you'd be happy to sell off the town. I can't believe they believed that."

"Well, we are taking her money," Grant reminded her. "For her damned soap commercial. I need to talk to Carter."

He made no move to jump up and go, however, which was fine with Christina. Grant was warm, naked, delectable, in a hot, gorgeous cowboy way. She could stay here with him all the rest of the afternoon and on into the night.

People at the diner had reminded Christina that Grant was a bad boy, always in trouble when he'd been younger. They thought that being nice to Karen meant he was still bad.

But they should know better. Grant was a Texas gentleman, raised to be courteous to a lady — any lady — even if she was a shark.

... And a bitch, and wore too much makeup, and had tried to jump Grant, and ...

Christina relaxed. Grant's body was around her, keeping her safe from the world. No need to disturb that.

Their conversation drifted to a close, but they didn't move to get up, leave, or talk about what had just happened between them.

The minute they did that, Christina knew, this bubble of serenity would break. Then she'd have to examine the pieces, see if she could fit it together again.

For now, Christina enjoyed touching Grant's shoulder, leaning to lick the hollow of his throat. Grant watched her in silence, touching her in response, their mouths meeting from time to time for quiet, warm kisses.

As the sun slipped down, Grant rolled her under him and slid gently inside her.

They made love, this time slowly, in warm contentment instead of crazed heat.

Contentment, that is, until their need built up, their bodies seeking more, then more. Finally Grant's thrusts came hard and fast, and Christina cried out, giving up on restraint.

Grant groaned her name, kissing her face, her throat. Christina wound higher, her arms coming around him to cling to his strong body. Grant braced himself on fists, his face set as he loved her in swift strokes.

A wave of pure joy broke over Christina, taking her down into darkness. She heard her voice, yet felt nothing but the hot wildness where they joined, Grant's fingers between them doing their magic.

Christina floated in a world that contained only the two of them, where nothing could ever hurt her.

"I need you, Christina," Grant was saying. "You are crazy, hot, and fucking *beautiful*."

He groaned out the last word, his eyes closing tightly. Christina held on, until they were both making a hell of a lot of noise, the bed — the whole damn room — rocking with their loving.

The sun sank and twilight began, and still they loved, until they fell, exhausted and shaking, into each other, and held on like they'd never let go.

***

Someone pounded on the door. Grant jerked awake, growling.

Christina lay next to him, tangled in his sheets — still there, amazingly — but someone wanted to come inside in the worst way.

Grant rolled off the bed, grabbed his jeans and yanked them on, not bothering to locate his underwear in the dark.

He snapped on the kitchen light, blinking at the glare, and wrenched open the front door.

Carter stood on the step, his hazel eyes light green in the dusk. He took in Grant's disheveled state, and his gaze grew colder.

Right, like Carter had never had himself a wild afternoon. "What?" Grant snapped.

Carter tried to look past him. "Damn it, Grant, don't tell me you have her in here."

"Have who in here?"

"Karen. You disappeared with her after lunch. She didn't come back to the ranch, and the whole town's buzzing."

Grant's trailer was a few miles out of town, on the road leading south. If Karen had driven straight back to Fredericksburg, there was a chance no one in Riverbend had seen her go.

The bedroom door slammed open and Christina strode out, fully dressed.

"He's not with Karen," she declared. "He's with me. Has been with me all afternoon. Having sex. On his bed."

Not much could faze Carter Sullivan, but he blinked a few times, his angry look vanishing. Christina was clearly not what he'd expected.

"Sorry," Carter said. "I wouldn't have charged over here if I'd known."

"This wasn't exactly planned," Christina said. "But we're done. I'll go, and you two can yell at each other all you want."

"No!" Grant barked out the word before he could stop it. He put his arm across the doorway. "Don't go yet. Carter, give us a minute, will you?"

Carter looked at them both then nodded and put on his hat. "Come up to the house when you're ready," he said to Grant.

He gave Christina a polite nod, then turned and strode from the step to his truck, the moonlight glinting on the deep black of it. Grant closed the door.

Christina was right behind him, big purse in hand. "I really need to go. See you, Grant."

"Hold on a sec," Grant said in a firm voice. "What are you rushing away for?"

"I have a job, and I'm late. It's not fair to the others if I don't show up on time."

"Wait. Stay." Grant moved his hand from the door to touch her cheek. "I mean, when you're done with work, come back here. Stay with me."

Christina was already shaking her head. "I've been moving into Bailey's place. Have a lot of boxes and stuff I still need to haul over there ..."

"You know what I mean." Grant let his hand drop to his side. "Move in with me again."

Christina stared at him, vast pain flickering in her eyes. "Because we had sex today? Neither of us could help that. It doesn't mean we're ready to have another relationship." Her voice went soft, wistful. "We were always so bad at it before."

Grant knew she was right. "I know, baby, but I'd like to try."

She studied the carpet, or maybe his bare toes. "But really, what's changed?"

"I don't know." Grant's throat hurt. "Nothing. Everything."

"I hate this." Christina looked up at him, her eyes so full of fear that Grant touched her shoulder. "I hate being without you. But I can't go through it again. Us fighting all the time, trying our best to hurt each other, because ..." She stopped there, not wanting to talk about the elephant in the room. "Then breaking up. I can't face the pain of that again. I barely made it the last time."

"Yeah, I know. Me too." Grant caressed under the strap of her tank top, getting lost in the soft feel of her. "Maybe we should start all over again, you know? I could come to the bar, feed you that lame line I did when I was twenty-one and cocky as hell."

Christina's tiny smile almost broke him. "You mean when I took one look at you and got hot all over? You were one hunkalicious cowboy that night, smiling at me. I almost climbed over the bar and went for you. I'm as bad as Karen."

Grant warmed. "Really? You liked what you saw?" Then he thought about her exact words, and his ego deflated "Wait a minute, are you saying I'm old and saggy now?"

The corners of her eyes crinkled. "No. I meant that was the first time I'd seriously looked at you. You weren't just Adam Campbell's screw-up younger brother."

"So there's hope for me. How about I come to the bar one of these nights and ask you out again? And we'll take it from there."

Christina shook her head. "You always have everything figured out. What are you going to do if I say no?"

"Ask you again. And again. Until you say yes."

She raised her brows and put one hand on her hip. "Stalk me, you mean?"

Grant pretended to consider, and nodded. "Yep. If that's what it takes."

Christina lost her teasing look and reached for the door. This time Grant moved aside, gesturing that she was free to leave.

Christina turned back on the doorstep. "If Carter doesn't kill you tonight," she said slowly, "then sure, pull your line on me. But give me a couple days, all right? I want to be, you know ..."

She trailed off, but Grant understood. She wanted to be ready and not ready at the same time.

Grant hated to let her walk out. If he was into that tying-up bondage shit, he'd have her tethered to the bed already, waiting for him to get back from talking to Carter.

That image had his cock hardening and sweat beading on his forehead. Damn, he should *not* think about things like that.

Grant swung the door wider and kissed Christina quickly on the cheek. "Drive safe."

Christina gave him a startled look then nodded. "Good night."

"Night."

Christina drew a breath, squared her shoulders, and strode out.

Grant flipped on all the outside lights and came out and watched her walk to her car — in case coyotes ambushed her or something, he guessed. Or jackrabbits. There were a lot of those in the open field behind his house.

Christina got into her truck, cranked it on, and turned on the lights. A couple of jackrabbits raised their heads at the beams, then took off, rustling back into the grass.

Christina turned the truck and drove past Grant, giving him a look but not a wave, heading around the drive to the road.

Her taillights flashed as she braked, then faded as she drove from dirt to asphalt. A rush of engine, and she was gone.

Grant watched her, hope in his heart, as her truck's lights winked out on the other side of the hill.

Then he realized. "Aw, *shit!*"

Carter expected him at the house, but Grant's truck was already there, since he'd ridden with Tyler from the ranch to the train and then back to town with Karen. He was stranded.

Damn it to hell.

He could call someone at the house to come get him, but they'd laugh their asses off. Probably already were.

Grant went inside, redressed, combed his hair, then set off the couple of miles to the ranch on foot.

***

Carter Sullivan was working through dinner in the ranch's office at the stables, when a plate of sandwiches landed next to his elbow, along with a frosty glass of iced tea.

He looked up to see Grace Malory, her green eyes warm, taking a step back.

The high-ceilinged office had walls of polished wood, the one lamp on Carter's desk throwing a small glow in the big room. Grace stood in the shadows, light catching in her dark hair.

"Thought you might like something," she said. "Your mom made only enough dinner for Faith and herself tonight, since everyone else was out."

"Yeah."

Carter fought the sudden shyness that welled up inside him, the same shyness he'd battled as a kid. He used to go out and get himself into trouble to compensate for how it made him feel. He'd conquered the shyness a while back, or so he'd thought, except whenever Grace Malory walked into a room.

She was an astonishingly beautiful woman. And untouchable to someone like Carter, born on the wrong side of the tracks. Hell, those tracks were in entirely the wrong town.

Grace Malory was from an old ranching family who owned whole sections of land in River County. She'd been a debutante in a pretty white dress, then gone to college to major in culinary arts. She'd grown up clean and wholesome, while Carter was exactly the opposite—a foster kid, in and out of juvie, adopted by the kind Mrs. Campbell, still rough about the edges as an adult, with tatts and an attitude.

Hence, Carter was brusque and tongue-tied around Grace. Didn't explain why he wasn't the same way around her sister, Lucy, but whatever.

"What are you doing here?" he asked abruptly.

Grace didn't look offended. "Helping out with some baking. Your mom wanted to send a bunch of stuff to Faith's youth group at church for their bake sale, but she ran out of time. Since I'm one of the overeducated and underemployed these days, I decided I could make a bunch of cupcakes and cookies for it. I'd have brought you a cupcake, but they have hot pink icing, really girly. Chocolate, though."

"Okay." It was all that would come out of Carter's mouth followed by a gruff, "Thanks."

Grace's nose wrinkled. "Your mom said you'd probably starve yourself out here, so I thought—sandwich. Easy to eat while you're working."

Double-decker, toasted bread, with lots of meat and cheese, and not too much lettuce. The woman must be able to read his mind.

"Thanks," Carter said again, trying to loosen his tongue. "You didn't have to."

"I know." Grace shrugged. "I felt like it. Well … good night."

"Night."

Why that was so hard to say, Carter didn't understand. When he'd been unable to shove out the right words as a kid, and other kids had laughed at him, Carter had simply jabbed a blade at their non-vital body parts. They'd shut up real quick.

He couldn't exactly do that to Grace, nor did he want to. He'd never hurt her—or let anyone else hurt her either.

Grace lingered, as though she wanted to say something else. Carter waited.

Her nose wrinkled again, and she gave a little laugh and shook her head. Then she turned around, walked out, and closed the door.

Carter let out his breath as the latch clicked. His palms were slick with sweat.

Fuck this. He was a grown man. Carter had gotten over stupid teenage crushes a long time ago, especially after that crazy bitch who'd been Faith's mother had thrust Faith at him and vanished into the dust.

He didn't get women.

Carter wasn't too messed up to eat the sandwich, though. It was seriously good.

"Hey." Grant strode in, bringing night wind and dust with him, reminding Carter that he'd asked Grant to come to the ranch. Took him a few moments to shut out the warmth of his encounter with Grace and remember why.

Grant was breathing hard, like he'd been running. He'd left his truck here, Carter had seen. The stupid-ass must have jogged from his trailer, too proud to ask for a ride. Carter had grown fond of his adoptive brothers over the years, but he still couldn't figure out why they did what they did.

"That looks good." Grant eyed the sandwich but didn't touch it, or the corn chips Grace had added to the plate.

When they'd been kids, Grant might have helped himself, and then Carter would have chased him down, and they'd have a fight. Carter had usually won the fights, unless Adam joined in, making it two on one.

Carter had learned to pull his punches, though — he'd grown up street fighting, which meant disabling your opponent quickly, no matter what it took. Either the other guy went to the hospital or you did.

It had taken him a few fights to realize that wrestling with brothers wasn't about truly hurting them. It was about dominance, learning lessons and, weirdly, friendship.

"Hands off," Carter said. "There's food up at the house."

Grant should have chuckled, remembering the old days, but he just stood there, thumbs on his belt buckle. He was dressed, hair combed, but it was so obvious he'd spent all afternoon and evening in bed it wasn't funny.

"About Christina ..." Grant said slowly.

"What about her?" Carter asked when Grant stopped. "You guys back together?"

"No." Grant said the word too quickly. "I mean, I don't know. Do me a favor, and don't talk about it with anyone."

Carter shot him an annoyed look. He didn't gossip. "Who am I going to tell?"

"Mom. Faith. Ross. Tyler. Adam ..."

"It's your business, and Christina's. I won't say a word."

Grant lifted his hands. "All right, all right. What did you want that had you coming to my trailer instead of calling?"

"I did call." Carter leaned back in his chair, lacing his hands behind his head. "You didn't answer, so I figured you lost your phone again. What happened with Karen today?"

"I took her out to lunch, and we talked about the script," Grant answered easily. "Then she tried to jump my bones, then she went home."

Chapter Ten

Okaaay, Carter thought. "Christina interrupt you?"

"What?" Grant looked harassed. "No. Christina ... It's complicated." He drew a breath. "Christina came to tell me that Karen wants to buy up Riverbend. Did you know that?"

Carter gave him a nod. "I only found out myself this evening. Mom said they made an offer on Circle C as well, and told me everyone saw you and Karen drive out toward your trailer. That's why I came down."

Grant balled his fists. "How could we be the last to know? Apparently, everyone in the diner was talking about it."

"I don't know. I've been focused on the commercial, and fifty other things this ranch is doing at the same time. I don't have my ear to the ground about the real estate market."

Carter spoke calmly, but anger rolled around inside him, the rage of the youth who'd been pulled from place to place, never able to control where he went. Hearing that someone wanted to buy Riverbend, and Circle C Ranch, his sanctuary, smacked him in the gut.

"Mom said no, right?" Grant asked.

Carter gave him a look. "What do you think? But if Karen's company succeeds, Riverbend is gone."

"And we'll be surrounded by housing developments and shopping malls and golf courses, right?"

"Yes," Carter said tightly.

Grant looked as unhappy as Carter felt. "What the hell can we do about it? We could buy up all the land ourselves—do we have that kind of money?"

"Not that kind," Carter said. "And it's more complicated than that. The developers are wooing the town council with all the money they'll bring in when new people move here. The council will try to get current buildings condemned or writs served on owners to either fix up their property or pay so much in fines they're forced to sell."

"They can't do that," Grant said indignantly. "Can they?"

"'Fraid they can." Carter didn't like government or politics, having had to deal with the law enforcement part of it so much. But he'd learned that officials could be more corrupt than the nastiest drug dealer, all while they went to church on Sunday and helped out at the school.

"Well, we can't just sit around and wait for the bulldozers," Grant growled. "Some of the people around here have nowhere to go. Hell, *we* have nowhere else to go."

"I've been thinking about this," Carter said. "I'm betting we can stop them by keeping Karen Marvin happy."

Grant opened his mouth to argue, then closed it. Carter watched thoughts go through his brother's head, churning them as he rearranged his ideas. "Okay," Grant said. "What does that mean?"

"Karen isn't the only person in her development company," Carter answered. "Her ex-husband, for one, is the CEO, but she has a lot of pull, a lot of influence with the board of directors, from what I've found out. If we show her the real Riverbend, get her to know the people here, and get her to like the town, she might not want to ruin it."

Grant looked skeptical. "This is your great idea?"

"It worked in the neighborhoods when I was a kid. If someone moved in and tried to take over, we got him to like it there, to protect the place instead of just gut it." Carter paused. "It didn't always work, but mostly, it did. People like places where they feel welcome, at home, respected. Even gang lords."

"If you say so." Grant frowned at him, blue eyes troubled, angry.

"Karen can be won to our side and help us," Carter went on. "Or she could walk away and not care. I prefer to keep her happy. Was she mad at you for not sleeping with her?"

Grant shook his head. "Didn't seem like it. But I'm going to tell you this right now, Carter." He leaned on his fists on the desk. "I'm not going to make myself a man-whore to save Riverbend.

Someone else can throw themselves on that grenade."

"I didn't think you would."

"Then what do you want me to do?" Grant unclenched his fists and dropped into a leather chair on the other side of the desk.

"Just make sure Karen's pleased with us. Wine her, dine her, take her to the bar. Find her a cowboy to hit the sack with, if that's what she's into. Butter her up."

"Meanwhile, the whole town wants to lynch me for consorting with the enemy."

"She won't be the enemy if we do this the right way."

Grant let out another growl. "Sure. Then you can take all the knives out of my back, but I might already be dead. Why can't *you* wine and dine her?"

"Because I know fuck-all about wine and food," Carter said. "You know the spots to go. So does Christina. Ask her to help you."

"Wait, wait, wait a minute. You want me ..." Grant pointed at his chest..."to ask my ex-girlfriend—the woman I want more than anything to get back into my life—to help me woo a shark of a woman, so we can save our hometown?"

"You got it."

Grant shot him an irritated look. "You make it sound so easy."

"It is easy. You're good at this, Grant."

"Yeah, but why *me*? Why not Tyler? Or Ross? Ross can be her cowboy-cop fantasy. Women like that."

"Because Karen likes *you*. She told me so."

Grant shook his head. "What she wants is another notch in her bedpost."

Carter sat back again. "You're chased by women all the time. It's never bothered you before. Usually you lap it up."

"Not the same thing at all. And if I'm going to have another chance with Christina, I don't want other women anywhere near me. I'll become a monk if that's what it takes."

"Might defeat the purpose," Carter said dryly. "Tell Christina what's going on. She's not stupid. She might be willing to help."

"Yeah, right." Grant got to his feet with restless energy. "You're crazy. Think I'll go on up to the house and find something to eat."

Carter shrugged. Grant would have to come at this in his own way. He always did.

"Grant." When Grant paused at the door and gave Carter an inquiring look, Carter said, "Don't screw it up with Christina this time. I think it will be your last chance."

Carter didn't miss the pain in Grant's eyes, a pain that ran deep. "Thanks, bro. You sure know how to make me feel better."

"Hey, I got your back."

Grant snorted something, banged out, and slammed the door.

***

Carter ate the sandwich, one of the best he'd ever had. He spent another hour finishing up the accounts, shut everything down, and carried the empty plate back with him to the house.

Grant had already gone—he pulled out in his truck as Carter left and locked the office. Grant lifted his hand in farewell, and drove away.

Grace Malory, on the other hand, was in the kitchen, doing the dishes.

Carter halted in the kitchen doorway, plate in hand, ready to fade silently into the hall and head for his suite in the back of the house. He'd get rid of the plate somewhere along the way.

But his daughter, Faith, sat at the kitchen table, doing homework. She heard Carter and looked up. "Hi, Daddy. I saved you a cookie."

Grace turned around, wet to her elbows, and gave him her crinkle-nosed smile. "She wanted to wait for you."

Carter made his feet move into the kitchen and head for the sink. Numbly he started to put the empty plate on the counter.

Grace reached for it and grabbed on to the edge. Carter felt the pressure of her hand through the plate, and the shy lump wedged itself in his throat.

Grace tugged, brows coming together when Carter wouldn't release the plate. She tugged again, a little harder.

Carter abruptly let go, and Grace took a staggering step back. Carter reached out to steady her, but Grace had already turned nimbly away.

Faith giggled. "That was funny."

"Plate dancing," Grace said, her back to them as she scrubbed.

Carter moved to the table and sat down, out of breath for some reason. Faith was writing numbers on a piece of paper.

"Math homework?" he asked, for something to say.

"Trying to figure out how much we should sell the cookies and cupcakes for to make enough money for the youth group." Faith bent her head over the numbers again, the kitchen light glistening on the dark ponytail that hung between her slender shoulder blades. Her small fingers worked the pencil over the paper. "Not so high people won't buy them but not so little we don't have any profit. We should also offer two for a little bit of a bargain, an incentive to buy more." She looked up at Carter, her hazel eyes clear.

Carter blinked. She was his little girl all right. "Sounds good," he said.

Faith pushed a plate of mostly crumbs over to him. On its center was one roundish chocolate chip cookie. "Three different kinds of chocolate in it," Faith said. "I wouldn't let Grace put the nuts in this batch. I don't like them with nuts, and I know you don't either."

When Carter only looked at the cookie, Faith pushed the plate closer. "So *try* it."

Carter lifted the cookie and took a bite. An amazing flavor sensation hit his mouth—buttery, chocolaty, sweet but not too sweet, with a hint of caramelized brown sugar.

"'S good," he said.

"Told you." Faith gave him a triumphant look. "I could only save you one, because the rest are for the bake sale. But Grace said she'd make more another time." Faith tapped the notepad with her pencil. "I think she should open a bakery."

Grace said from the sink, "Have to have money to do that. I'm fresh out, right now. But maybe someday." Carter heard the sad resignation in her voice.

She wiped up all the counters, dried her hands, and joined them. "I'm heading home. Pick you up tomorrow, Faith, around nine?" Grace glanced at Carter when she said the time, making sure this was all right with Faith's dad.

Carter was already rising to his feet. That's what a gentleman did when a woman was leaving, Olivia had drilled into him.

"Yeah, that's fine." Carter said. He almost said, *Wait, tomorrow's school,* before he remembered the next day was Saturday. His brain always moved slower around Grace.

"Okay, then." Grace tilted her head, studying Carter. "You have chocolate, just there." She pointed to the corner of her lower lip.

Carter snatched up a paper napkin from the table and scrubbed his mouth.

"Good night," Grace said. "Again."

Carter nodded, still wiping. "G'night."

Grace leaned down to kiss Faith on the top of her head, lifted a tote bag from a chair, and walked out the kitchen door into the dark.

Carter dumped the paper napkin and went out after her. Things were pretty safe around here, but he waited, in the shadows beyond the circle of the porch light, to make sure she made it to her car all right. He knew to stand in the dark, so predators wouldn't see him, until it was too late for them.

Grace, oblivious, got into her car, started it, and drove smoothly away. Carter watched until he couldn't see her anymore, then he returned to the house.

Faith was doodling on her notepad, her dark head down. "You liiiike herrr," she said softly.

Carter didn't respond. He'd only make a fool of himself if he did. "Come on," he said. "It's time for bed."

Faith never fussed about going to bed. She said she liked to lie in the dark and make up stories in her head. She was a fearless kid, which Carter always marveled at. He'd spent his young years in terror.

Faith caught up her notepad and pen and took Carter's hand to lead him down the hall. Carter reached back, grabbed the second half of the cookie, and stuffed it into his mouth as he went.

These really were damn good.

***

The bar was crowded on Saturday night, like it was supposed to be. Christina pulled taps, poured wine, and occasionally mixed drinks, though this was more a beer scene.

Grant walked in with Karen Marvin. As had happened at the restaurant, everyone looked, went stone-faced, and then returned to conversations, voices subdued.

Tyler and Ross were the only ones who greeted him, and he nodded at them in return. Karen was clinging to Grant like a limpet to a boat she particularly liked. Grant, as though he didn't notice, walked her up to the bar, taking off his hat.

Grant looked good. His button-down shirt was smooth across his shoulders and abs, jeans hugged his thighs, and his rolled-up sleeves showed off well-muscled forearms.

The other bartender, Rosie, tried to move past Christina to take the order, knowing the awkwardness between Christina and Grant. Christina stepped in front of her, giving her a look that said it was all right.

"Hey, Grant," Christina said in a pleasant voice. "What can I get you?"

Grant's eyes flickered, and Christina kept her neutral expression in place. She'd be nice. At least for now.

"What will you have, Karen?" Grant asked, polite and attentive.

Karen rested her hands on the bar. "Do you have a Burgundy? Nothing too aromatic. A light grape."

"We do," Christina said. "But it's crap, trust me. I make a mean cosmo, though."

Karen pursed her lips. She wore pale pink lipstick that went with her subdued eye shadow and carefully mascaraed lashes. She wore a black business suit with a brief skirt, which showed off shapely legs, her blond hair in a neat bun.

Christina contrasted her with the buckle bunnies Grant had brought in here the night before Bailey's wedding. Karen had far better taste clothes and makeup, but she hung on to Grant just as hard.

"I don't like anything too sweet," Karen said after considering. "How about a dry martini?"

"Can do. Grant? Can I get you a martini as well?"

Grant thought mixed drinks were a sign of the apocalypse. He shook his head so fast Christina couldn't stop her grin. "Just a beer," he said. "You know what I like."

"Coming up."

Christina put down two square napkins and bent to mixing the martini. She was good at it, putting in just enough gin, not too much vermouth. Christina popped in an olive on a stick, set the drink carefully on Karen's napkin, and got out a mug.

She opened a bottle of the brand of beer Grant hated most and poured it into the glass, making a picture-perfect head.

"There y'all are. Enjoy."

Grant gave her a dark look, which Christina returned blandly. "How's the commercial going?" she asked.

Karen answered after taking a demure sip of her martini. "We haven't started yet. But the train looks good, doesn't it, Grant? They'll be able to do their stunts on it, so they say."

"Sure," Grant said. "Tyler's got a lot of good ideas."

"I look forward to seeing them," Karen said. "These gentlemen can ride, can't they?" she asked Christina.

"We've been watching them do it since they were kids," Christina answered, as amiable as Karen.

Blah, blah, blah.

What Karen was really saying was, *Sorry, sweetie, you had your chance.*

To which Christina would reply, *Eat it, woman. This is not what it looks like.*

Grant had called Christina and told her what Carter had relayed to him last night. After Christina got over the double shock of Grant being able to find his phone and then Grant *calling* her, she'd settled down to listen.

I'm drawing the line at helping her get into bed with you, Christina had said. *My loyalty to Riverbend only goes so far.*

Darlin', I'd rather get into bed with a coral snake. Be a faster way to go.

I don't know, Christina had said. *I can be kind of a viper.*

Grant had chuckled, that low, warm sound. *No, honey, you're a sugar bear.*

And he'd hung up.

The words had warmed her all afternoon, even when she'd watched Karen walk in, fixed to his side.

"How about we go join your brothers?" Karen asked Grant, done conversing with Christina.

"All right." Grant took up his beer, looked at it, set it down again. As Karen turned away, Grant said to Christina. "Give that to someone thirsty. Twenty minutes, all right? Then you come rescue me."

"Is *that* all it takes you these days?" Christina said. She didn't touch the beer.

Grant pointed a finger at her. "You are so asking for it."

Christina only gave him a little smile and let him walk away.

Chapter Eleven

"This is our baby brother, Ross," Grant told Karen.

Karen gave Ross, who wore civilian clothes of black shirt and jeans, a once-over. "The deputy," she said archly. "*Very* pleased to meet you."

She held out her hand and squeezed Ross's when he shook it. Ross's brows went up the tiniest bit.

Knew it, Grant thought. *She's into the cowboy cop thing.*

Ross curled his hand back and put it on his lap. "You not drinking anything, Grant?"

Karen looked around. "Oh, you left your beer on the bar. I'll have your little barmaid bring it over."

Grant caught her hand before she could raise it. "It's fine. Did you enjoy the bake sale?"

Karen's straight-toothed smile flashed. "Yes, it was the cutest thing." To his brothers' surprised looks, she said, "Grant took me to an actual bake sale at your church. Where people *baked* things and sold them to raise money. This town is just adorable."

Tyler looked mystified. "Yeah, we like it."

"Then, honey, we have to keep my ex from ruining it," Karen said.

The three of them stopped. "Your ex?" Tyler asked carefully. Carter had filled him in about Karen's ex but the brothers waited to hear what she had to say.

"Preston Waters, the Third." Karen took a sip of her martini. "He owns a development company with me. He wants to do a master-planned community out here. Part of why I'm here is I promised to check it out. Personally, I think he's an idiot."

The people at the next table, hearing this last statement, turned in their direction. They said nothing, but swung away to talk to each other. And to the next table. The gossip machine cranked to life.

"I hear he wants to buy up a lot of land," Grant said casually. "Including the middle of town."

"Preston wants to buy the world and make it his own," Karen said. She wrinkled her face, her makeup creasing before smoothing out again. "That's all he cares about. Why do you think I dumped him? The *I'm a hot, rich, successful businessman* thing got old real fast. I've turned into a more down-home kind of gal."

She caressed Grant's wrist, while Tyler and Ross concentrated on their drinks, faces contorting as they tried not to bust up laughing.

"He's sure that people will rush out here and buy a suburban home seventy miles from anywhere." Karen shrugged slender shoulders. "He might be right, but I think he'll be disappointed. I predict he'd have about one-third sell-through and then be stuck with all those properties and all those new houses no one wants. Seen it happen before. Would be a shame."

A real shame, Grant thought. Land got overbought and overbuilt, and the people the developers counted on buying the individual places didn't come. Communities disappeared and people were scattered, for nothing.

"Preston's already got irons in the fire." Karen stirred her drink. "So it's moving forward. I'd love to see him fall on his ass, even though a lot of my money's tied up in it too. I'd like to thwart him by buying up the real estate out from under him, but I don't have the money."

"Maybe we can have another bake sale," Tyler suggested, his face straight.

Karen gave him a wry look. "Aw, ain't you sweet. But I *could* do something like that, you know. Maybe have you boys put on a show, to raise money to buy up the town yourselves."

Grant drummed his fingers on the table. "We already own the town. I mean, the properties already have owners who live here."

"True, but the mortgage company has bought up a lot of loans, and on some places, the ownership is under question. I'm very good at chaining a piece of property. Ownership can be convoluted. This bar, for instance." She looked around.

"Christina's uncle owns it," Grant said. "Sam Farrell."

"You sure about that?" Karen asked. "Because I have a report that says he doesn't."

Grant stared at her. "Can't be right. He's run it forever."

Karen gave him a patient look. "Sam Farrell hasn't *owned* this place in three years. He took out a second mortgage, and then got way behind on the payments. The bank in town took the bar, but the head of the bank — Mr. Carew is it? — lets Sam lease it and keep running it. There was a letter stating that Sam planned to buy the place back sooner or later, but he's not done it so far."

Tyler raised his brows. "Does Christina know this?" he asked Grant.

Grant shrugged, worried. "If she does, she's never mentioned it."

Karen glanced at Christina, who was smiling at Kyle Malory while she poured him a beer, probably not one he hated.

"Maybe she's embarrassed," Karen said. "It's another old-school value I don't have — thinking it's vulgar to talk about money."

Grant watched Christina leaning on her arms to talk to Kyle in a friendly way. His heart burned. She was so beautiful, and it drove him crazy when she turned that beauty on other guys, especially when they were Malorys.

"Christina doesn't embarrass easy," Grant said absently as he watched her. "If she knew, she would have said something to *someone*."

"Oh, well." Karen took another delicate sip of her martini. She wasn't the kind to down alcohol until she was roaring drunk, it seemed. No getting her sloshed and making her sign papers stating she wouldn't destroy the town. "The bank is willing to sell the bar if Sam can't buy it back. Preston, the total bastard, has put a bid on it, but I made a personal one. Now all we have to do is see who wins."

***

Christina waited exactly twenty minutes, then waited another five, because she wanted Grant to sweat a little. Then she walked out from behind the bar, making her way to the Campbells' table.

When she was within two yards of them, Grant rose, excused himself, leaving his hat, and caught Christina by the arm.

"Take a break."

"What?" Christina refused to jerk away, because that story would be all over town. Well, it would be all over town anyway, but she'd rather not have people saying that she and Grant were fighting in the middle of the bar.

"Take a break," he repeated. "I need to talk to you."

Grant's brows were drawn, his look serious. Christina stopped the argument before it reached her lips and let him escort her out the back door.

Once outside, Grant kept walking, away from the Dumpsters and the sour smell of trash, out to where the lot ended in a hedge dividing it from the road. In the relatively cool, green-scented night, Grant stopped.

"What?" Christina said, worried. "Everything all right? Something wrong with Bailey …?"

Grant put his fingers to her lips. "No, baby. Sorry, I didn't mean to scare you."

"Then what's up?"

She didn't want to be out here in the dark with him, not when he looked so good, smelled so good.

The dim lights made his eyes a deep blue. She didn't trust herself with him at all.

"I'm just going to ask this," Grant was saying. "Did you know your uncle sold this place? About three years ago?"

Christina stared, the words making no sense. "What are you talking about? Who told you that? Wait, I bet it was Miz Ice Queen."

"Yeah, she did. But she had no reason to lie about it. It's easy enough to prove."

Christina took a few steps away from him. Sam had sold the bar? Without telling her? He'd never do that. Karen had to be feeding Grant bullshit.

Sam had always said that, because he and Christina's aunt Caroline had never had any kids, Christina would inherit the bar and the land it was on when Sam was gone. A little nest egg for her. While she hadn't pinned her financial hopes on inheriting the place, Christina didn't believe Sam would turn around and sell it without ever saying a word.

"That can't be true," Christina said with conviction. "Karen's lying. Or, I'll be generous and say she's mistaken."

Grant's slow shake of his head shot worry through her. "Sam didn't have a choice, it sounds like. He owed big time on a loan, and the bank took it as collateral." He let out his breath. "I suspected you didn't know. I guess he didn't tell anyone, and Carew at the bank is his friend. He'd keep it quiet too."

Christina stared as Grant's words penetrated. Dear God, it really was true. Sam had let the bank foreclose on the bar ... "And he didn't *tell* me?" she finished out loud. "What the hell? I could have helped him, damn it. Why didn't he say anything?"

She knew Grant didn't know — her anger and worry was simply spilling out.

"He probably had had his reasons," Grant said. "I'm guessing pride being one of them."

Christina huffed a breath. "*Pride?* What the hell …?"

But then, that was her uncle all over. Her father was like that too. They'd been raised to believe that, when they were in trouble, they turned aside and solved the problem themselves, instead of upsetting people close to them. Aunt Caroline had been like that too, never talking about her heart disease with anyone but Sam until she was in the hospital, dying from it. Christina hadn't even known she'd been sick. She remembered her grief, and her fury, when she'd found out. This was more of the same. *Damn* him.

"I need to talk to Sam," Christina said with heat. "And if all this is true, I need to kick his ass."

Grant regarded her quietly, his large strength too comforting. "So what if it is true? He still runs the place. He still cuts your checks. Karen says that if she buys it, she'll cut him a deal and pay Sam to keep running it. Your uncle won't have to worry about money anymore, and you'll still have your job."

"If *Karen* buys it?" Christina's eyes widened. "She wants to buy the bar?"

"That's what she said. To keep her ex from having it. But at least she wants to keep it going, not tear it down."

Christina's body went cold, and she spun away, unable to keep still. "Oh, that's just perfect," she said to the sky. "There is no *way* I can work for that woman. I don't care if she runs back to Houston and lets her company flatten the town. I am *not* running drinks for the bitch who was crawling all over my boyfriend."

Christina turned in her agitated pacing to find Grant right in front of her.

"Your boyfriend?" he asked, voice soft, eyes dark.

"You know what I mean."

"No, I don't think I do. Are you saying we're back together?"

Yes. No. Christina waved her arms. "I don't know what I'm saying."

Grant's anger flashed in his face. "*I'm* saying you're the one who sailed over to my house and hid in my bedroom. Was it just for playtime? Or to get my hopes up?"

"I didn't do that on purpose," Christina said, exasperated. She remembered her panic, her embarrassment as she dove into the closet. "I went there to warn you about Karen, remember? I didn't realize you'd be bringing her home with you so she could attack you on the kitchen counter."

Grant's look was hard. "If you needed to talk to me so bad, why didn't you go come find me at the ranch? Or leave a message with my mom or Carter?"

Which Christina could have done. He was right— she'd gone to the trailer because she'd wanted to be alone with Grant. She'd even admitted that to herself when she'd been there.

"I don't know!" Christina's face went hot. "None of that matters right now. I'm just saying I can't work for a woman who is imagining going down on you in the back seat of her expensive car. What do I know? She might have done it already."

Grant glared. "I haven't touched her. I told you. I don't want her."

Christina wasn't sure why she was getting so mad right now about … well, everything. The shock of her uncle losing the bar, Karen wanting it, and Grant trying to pin her down on what she felt, poked red-hot needles into her brain.

Words welled up and blasted out before Christina could stop them. "Well, maybe you should leave a sticker on the ones you *do* want! So we'll all know. What do you think it's like for me seeing you with all these women? You had *three* of them the night before the wedding. You were kissing them, letting them fondle you, calling them *sweetheart.*"

"Christina, you know those buckle bunnies are just part of the show."

The Campbell boys always said that. Tyler usually said it while he had his arms draped around two women's shoulders, one twining a leg around his, the other's hand moving to his ass. Cowboys were expected to have hot women in tight clothes all over them, especially show cowboys like Grant and his brothers.

When they'd been dating, Grant had made sure the only woman people saw with him had been Christina. As soon as they'd split up, he'd joined in with the "part of the show" philosophy.

Christina had told herself she was okay with it—it was Grant's life, and they weren't together anymore.

But now every single instance rose up and twisted around in her heart.

"*They* don't know they're part of the show," Christina said heatedly. "You could have some pride, or at least some consideration. Everyone's laughing their asses off at me. And you."

Grant's fists balled, his face flushing. "What the hell am I supposed to do? Take a vow of celibacy in front of the whole town because the only woman I ever loved walked out on me?"

The only woman I ever loved...

While Christina's mouth popped open in stunned surprise, Grant dragged in a breath and went on. "And how do you think *I* feel seeing you driving back from Ray Malory's place at the crack of dawn, still in your bridesmaid's gown? *I* didn't get laid that night, but you sure did."

Christina slammed herself to him, where she could yell right into his face. "I drove Ray home, because he was plastered, and I didn't want to leave him alone. I told you, I broke up with him!"

"After you gave him one last horizontal tango, like you did with me?"

"No, I *didn't*. And why do you keep saying *I* left *you*? I moved out, yeah, but you're the one who shoved me out the door!"

"What the hell are you talking about?" Grant roared. "You couldn't run away fast enough!"

Christina balled her hands. "I remember you saying, *I can't stand looking at you and being reminded of every damn thing wrong between us. Sometimes I wish you'd just get the hell out.*" She stopped, the hurt of that striking her anew. "So, I got the hell out."

"And that is *not* what I meant!"

"Then why did you say it? I'm supposed to have an interpreter follow me around and explain what you do mean every time you yell at me?"

"Baby, you know I'm not good with words. I don't say them right."

Christina touched her clenched fists to his chest. "Not good enough. You had plenty of time to explain to me what you wanted. You helped me pack. You drove my stuff to my apartment. It wasn't like I was there one second and gone the next. It was days—weeks! And you never asked me to come back."

"Because I knew you needed time away from me. And I ..." Grant let out his breath. "I needed time away from you."

"You see? You *did* want me to get the hell out."

Grant thrust his hands through his hair, swinging away from her. "Aw, *damn* you. It always has to be *your* interpretation that's right, doesn't it?"

Christina darted around to face him again. "This is why I can't answer whether we're back together. Every time we're near each other, we fight. About everything. All the time. We accuse each other and then try to see who can hurt each other the worst."

"I know." Grant stilled, breathing hard. "I know, baby."

"I can't stay here." Christina ripped off the black bartender's apron she wore and threw it to the ground. "I have to go."

Grant said nothing for a moment, then he reached for her. "Wait a sec. Don't leave yet. Carter's got me doing a dance, remember? You're supposed to help me out."

Christina's job tonight had been to steer Karen to some red-hot cowboys who'd make all her wishes come true. Make her so interested in them she'd leave Grant and the Campbell boys alone.

Christina made a noise of exasperation. "I am *not* going back in there and sucking up to that woman. Tell Kyle, or someone, to introduce her around. In fact, I'm *never* going back in that bar again. I *quit!*"

"You're just going to walk away after all these years?" Grant snarled. "Oh, wait, that's what you always do."

Christina's rage boiled high. She was glad he'd chosen to be a shit about this—made it easier.

"That's it." She pointed both forefingers at Grant—who looked heartbreakingly good, damn him. "I'm done with *you*, and this job, and this whole damn town!" She swung around and stomped away, off into the quietness of the night.

She heard him say, "Christina, wait. I shouldn't have …" and drift to silence.

Christina knew if she turned around and looked at him, accepted his halfhearted apology, let him sweet-talk her again, she'd never go. She'd burst into tears, right in the middle of Second Street and stand there like a fool. She'd want everything she'd tried to have with Grant, everything that never worked before, and would never work again.

She kept walking.

"Christina." Grant's voice was low, growly, but Christina went on.

***

Christina heard nothing from Grant over the next couple weeks, which was fine with her.

The fight—stupid, stupid, just like all their fights—had drained her energy. She was furious with him, with her uncle, with Karen, with Riverbend. And with herself.

The best thing to do was lie low and think about her options.

She heard about Grant, though. She heard that Karen had hooked up with a couple guys at the bar that night who'd driven back to Fredericksburg with her. What had happened there, people could only speculate. Grant hadn't been with them.

Grant and his brothers went out and worked on the commercial shoot. They showed Karen around, they took her out, they were polite to her.

Word got around that Karen was trying to block her husband buying up Riverbend's properties, and people softened toward her. Since Karen seemed to be pretty smart, she probably knew the Campbell boys were trying to work on her, and she was eating it up with a spoon.

Christina didn't go back to work. She'd been able to save up money over the years, and she was finished with slinging drinks, a job that was supposed to have been temporary once upon a time while she decided what she wanted to do with her life. When her uncle had begged her to stay longer, she'd done it, to help him out.

She'd also stayed because of Grant. The job let her be close to him.

If not for Grant, she'd have left Riverbend long ago, she realized. She'd have gone to San Antonio with her parents or to Houston with Lucy and tried to start a career. She'd stayed for Grant, then for Bailey.

Now it was all gone. Sam had lied to her, Bailey had a new life, Grant and Christina had nothing left, and there was no reason for Christina to live here anymore.

So Christina told herself, though tears swam in her eyes every time she thought about packing up and driving away.

She went to see her Uncle Sam, a silver-haired man who stood as straight and tall now as he had when Christina had been little. It didn't take Sam long to look at Christina in sorrow and confess everything.

"Your aunt had just passed," he said. The two of them sat on his front porch on a Sunday afternoon, sipping iced tea and watching the sunshine on the bluebonnets. "I got into debt taking care of her, got behind on the property taxes and fees on the bar, and I mortgaged the place to pay for everything. Then when I couldn't pay on *that*, Carew came to see me. He had to take the bar, but let me keep running it for them, with an understanding I'd be buying it again when I could."

"But why didn't you tell my dad?" Christina asked. "Why didn't you tell *me*? We could have helped you."

"I know, angel. But I was grieving and ashamed. And don't take this the wrong way, but your dad always likes to have the upper hand with me, you know what I mean? Always has. I didn't want to go crawling to him and confess I lost the bar. Sometimes friends can help more than family. I'm sorry, sweetie."

Sam looked so dejected and forlorn that Christina reached over and squeezed his hand. "I understand," she said.

"Thanks, angel."

"I'm still not going back, though. I need a change—I've been putting it off for too long."

"And you don't want to work for Karen." Sam's lips twitched. "Don't blame you. I've met her."

"Can't you talk to Mr. Carew and tell him not to sell to her—to anyone?"

"Sure I can. But it's big money. Who am I to tell him he can't accept? He's getting older, like me. He and his wife deserve to retire and live half the year in Hawaii if they want. A big sale will help him do that."

Christina deflated. "Yeah."

There were always more than two sides to everything, she'd learned. Life was more complicated than black and white, good and evil.

She was still not happy with Sam for not telling her, but she understood. Choices were hard.

Sam's choices, on the other hand, had given Christina options. She talked to Lucy, who sounded excited that Christina was finally coming out to Houston. Lucy could introduce Christina around, and get her started in a job. A real job, with real hours. No more tending bar and babysitting drunks.

Once she'd settled things with Lucy, Christina told Bailey what she planned, in a long, tearful phone call. Bailey and Adam had finished their honeymoon trip and were heading back to California to work on the movie Adam was stunt coordinator for. Bailey's life was moving on.

So was Christina's. She was finally free to decide her fate—without obligations to Riverbend, without obligations to Grant. Amid the pain of deciding to let Grant go for good, Christina was eager to find out what road her life would take.

She packed up her things at Bailey's house—she and Bailey decided they'd keep the place as a refuge, renting it out when they could. No selling to developers.

Christina was so engrossed in getting ready to go that she lost track of the rest of her life. Two days before she was to drive to Houston, she realized what the exact date was.

Christina's monthly cycle was so regular that she and Bailey joked they could set their calendars by it. Christina had figured she'd be done before she drove to Houston so she wouldn't have to worry about it on the road, never fun.

And then she'd forgotten all about it. Christina woke up in the bedroom of Bailey's shotgun house early in the morning, blinking while it hit her that she was more than a week late.

Well, shit.

Chapter Twelve

If Christina went to the corner drugstore and bought a pregnancy test, everyone in River County would be discussing it over their next meal.

She asked a couple friends if they needed her to pick up anything for them in Austin and drove there, using the excuse that she was buying more supplies for her move to Houston.

At a large chain grocery store in a road off Mopac, she bought what she needed. Christina ran the errands for her friends at Central Market, put a packed gallon of Amy's Ice Cream in the cooler she'd brought with her, and headed back to Riverbend.

That night Christina went into her bathroom, opened the test box, fingers shaking, and went through with it. The test showed positive for pregnancy.

The emotions that battered Christina made her end up flat on her back in bed. First—euphoria.

She'd thought for so long she couldn't conceive. The colored stick in her bathroom told her otherwise.

She was going to have a baby. Christina hugged that knowledge to herself, tears of joy leaking from her eyes.

Then, vast confusion. From the timing, the child could be Grant's ... or it could be Ray's. She'd been with Ray right before he'd gone to Lubbock for his bull riding. Two weeks later, she and Grant ...

Christina and Grant had tried to have a baby for the last couple years they'd been together. They'd stopped using condoms, pills, or other means; it had been bare body-to-body, nothing in the way.

Nothing had happened. And they'd seriously tried. Day and night. When no baby came, it had created a hell of a lot of tension between them. They'd tried not to talk about it, but then keeping it bottled up had made it come out in nasty explosions. Finally it had been too much to take, and they'd splintered.

Now this. Christina laid her hands on her abdomen, sure she felt the spark of life there. It was incredible.

But if she and Grant hadn't succeeded before, what was to say they suddenly could now? That meant, odds were, that the baby was Ray's. Not good.

These days, a pregnant woman could find out who'd fathered the child inside her before it was born. Though Christina was vague about how the tests worked, she knew she wouldn't have to wonder very long.

However, if the baby turned out to be Ray's, that meant Christina got to tell Grant he was shooting blanks.

You could always, a little voice inside her whispered, *choose which one you want and pretend he's the father for sure.*

Christina knew instantly she couldn't. She'd never lie to her own kid, or to the potential dads. As much as she wanted the baby to be Grant's, she couldn't do that to Ray. It wasn't like Ray was an evil mass murderer or anything. And maybe somewhere down the road it would be important to be aware of the family medical history. Even more than that, child and father deserved to know about each other.

No, Christina would tell the truth, no matter how painful it would be for all concerned.

Next step, see a doctor, confirm the test. Decide what to do.

Christina put her hands over her face. She felt so alone—missed Bailey so much. Bailey would listen in that clear-headed way of hers, and tell her what to do. Though Bailey was the younger sister, she had a lot of wisdom.

Christina rolled over, found her cell phone, wiped her eyes, and called Bailey.

***

Christina was avoiding Grant, he knew. That hurt like hell, but Grant didn't push it. He'd heard about her plans for moving to Houston, and that hurt too, but she hadn't gone yet. He'd planned to corner her and talk her out of it, but then her next-door neighbor, Mrs. Kaye, had told Grant Christina had stopped her frantic packing. Maybe she'd had a change of heart.

He needed to make sure the change of heart stuck, and Christina stayed in Riverbend. He had a few ideas how to go about it.

When he found Christina eating alone at Mrs. Ward's one day after the lunch crowd had drifted away, Grant slid into a chair at her table without apology.

"Hey, how you doing?" he asked.

Christina finished up a plate of vegetables and started on a milkshake. Mrs. Ward made real milkshakes, thick and creamy, and flavored with things like salted caramel or malted milk balls.

"Fine," Christina said.

"People ask me about you at the bar." Grant dropped his hat to the empty chair next to him. "As though I know what's up with you."

"I'm glad they're concerned," Christina said crisply. "You can tell them I'm fine. I talked to Sam, and understand what happened. It's behind me."

"Mmm-hmm."

She was being more abrupt than usual. Christina had plenty of sass, but it was usually good-natured sass. She didn't go out of her way to hurt people.

Today, she sat shoveling the milkshake into her mouth as if Grant didn't exist. The way she licked whipped cream off the spoon—that had his heart pounding and his cock tightening.

"You still thinking about leaving town?" Grant asked her.

He wanted to reach over, rip the spoon from her hand, and feed her the whipped cream himself. Then he'd lean and lick the droplets from her lips.

"Haven't decided," Christina said, shrugging. "I want to be careful what I choose. I *was* going to

Houston, but I might go up to Dallas instead, see what's going on there."

Dallas. Not all the way across the country, but even so, some hours away.

"Who do you know in Dallas?" Grant demanded. She couldn't just go to another city where she didn't know anyone and wander around by herself. Dangerous. He wouldn't let her.

"I have a few friends there. Bailey knows some people too. I'll be fine."

She kept saying *fine*. As though, if she said it enough, it would be true.

"How's your shoot?" Christina asked, scooping up more milkshake.

Grant set his mouth. "Fine."

"Oh. Good."

They sat in silence a few minutes, but it wasn't companionable. Christina continued to eat, her spoon clinking on the inside of the tall glass.

"Why don't you come out and watch us?" Grant suggested, trying to soften his voice. "Maybe you can dress up and be one of the passengers on the train. I'll come by and rob you."

Christina would probably try to beat him off rather than tamely give up her handbag, but it might be fun.

"Can't. I just told you, I'm heading up to Dallas."

His throat tightened. "You mean right now? For how long?"

"Don't know. I'm going tomorrow to look around." Christina thunked down her spoon, the glass empty. "I don't have my whole life planned out to the minute, all right?"

Damn, she was touchy today. "Hey, I'm just asking, sweetheart. You shouldn't drive to Dallas alone. Take someone with you."

"I'll be—"

"Don't you dare say *fine*." Grant leaned toward her, trying to keep the few people left in the diner from hearing. "You're not fine. You're mad at me and at the town, and you're not thinking straight. Take Grace with you. Or another friend. I don't like you out driving around in a big city by yourself. It's dangerous."

Christina glared at him. "I'll think about it."

"Do more than think about it, baby."

Christina flinched at the word *baby*. She opened her mouth, probably to yell at him for saying it, when a presence stopped next to them. Grant looked up at the round face of Mrs. Ward, who was watching them patiently.

"You ate *all* of that?" she asked, looking at Christina's empty shake glass. "I guess not staying out all night working gave you back your appetite. You Farrell girls were always too thin."

Christina, who considered herself plump for some reason, gave her a smile. "I'm just hungry today. And it's delicious. Irresistible."

"I'm glad you like it, dear." Mrs. Ward put a paper check facedown by Christina's plate.

Grant snatched it up. "I got this."

Christina's glare came back. *"Grant."*

Mrs. Ward studied them both, then picked up Christina's empty plate and glass. "I'll let you two fight over that. Just drop it next to the register when you leave."

Grant reached for his wallet. Christina snatched at the check, but it was plucked from Grant's hand by well-manicured fingers. "Let me take care of it," Karen said. "My treat."

She gave Christina a false smile, an odd glitter in her eyes.

Christina sat back rigidly. "Very nice of you," she said. "Not necessary."

"Doesn't matter." Karen breezed on past, signaled to a waitress to meet her at the cash register, and handed her the slip.

"Damn it," Christina muttered.

"Let it go," Grant said. "She's trying to make friends. She can't help it if she's clueless."

"Oh, I think that woman knows *exactly* what she's doing." Christina shoved her chair back. "Nice talking to you, Grant. I'll think about asking Grace to come with me. You're right, it's a long drive and a big city. See ya round."

Christina turned and walked away from him, saying a sweet good-bye and thank you to Mrs. Ward.

"She sure is mad at me," Grant said when he caught up to Karen at the door. "No one can stay madder at me better than Christina."

"I think she has a lot on her mind," Karen said, again with the cryptic look. "Now, I have things to do. See you back at the ranch."

"Right." Grant gave her a nod and put on his hat. "See ya."

All the women in this town were acting strange today.

***

Christina was tossing the last things into her overnight bag when someone rapped sharply on the front door. She really didn't want company, but Christina left her bedroom and went to answer it.

Seeing Grant had only made her acutely aware of the many things she needed to tell him. She didn't want to have that talk, though, until she was one-hundred percent sure she was pregnant, and two-hundred percent sure she knew who the father was.

After that, she'd leave it up to Ray or Grant to decide what they wanted to do. Christina was having the baby, and she wanted the baby to have a father, but she wouldn't trap either man into a marriage or relationship they didn't want. It would be their choice.

The knocking continued. Christina quickened her pace and yanked open the front door.

She caught Karen in the act of raising her hand to knock again.

"Hello, Christina," Karen said in her smooth voice. "I think we need to talk, don't you?"

Christina didn't open the door any wider. She'd been brought up to be hospitable even to the last person she wanted to see on her doorstep, but her patience had run out.

"What about?" she asked abruptly.

"You're going to want to let me in." Karen's smile was fixed. "So the neighbors won't overhear."

These older houses had been built very close together, with only a narrow strip of yard between each. Mrs. Kaye next door liked to work on the rose bushes that lined her property and keep an eye on her neighbors at the same time. Sure enough, she was there today, clipping, dead-heading, pretending not to notice Karen on the porch ten feet away from her.

"All right," Christina said. "Come on in."

Mrs. Kaye straightened up, pruning shears in hand, and watched interestedly as Karen waltzed into Christina's house and shut the door.

Chapter Thirteen

"What do we need to talk about?" Christina asked impatiently.

Karen wandered the room, taking in the photos on the shelves—Bailey's and Christina's both—which Christina hadn't been able to bring herself to pack yet. A house without photos was empty, forlorn, no longer hers.

"Your visit to Dallas." Karen skimmed off her white linen suit coat and laid it over the back of a chair. She wore a black sleeveless dress underneath. "I have to go up there too. You should let me drive you."

Christina was very sure she didn't want to spend three hours in a car with Karen. "No, it's all right. I'm going to ask Grace to go with me."

"Honey, you know you're not taking Grace. I can keep my mouth shut, trust me. I agree with Grant that you shouldn't go alone."

Christina stared, her body numb. "What are you talking about?"

"Your appointment with the ob-gyn. That's why you're going up to Dallas, isn't it?"

Christina's mouth went dry, but Karen only looked at her, waiting for an answer. "How the hell do you know that?" Christina asked, voice a croak.

"Because I saw you when you came back from Austin. I happened to be passing when you were delivering bags of whatever to your friend Rosie. Before you went up to her house, you took things out of the bags in your trunk and put them into your purse. I glimpsed the pregnancy test—I recognized the box. Have used it a time or two myself. Then you suddenly want to go to Dallas. I put it together that you wanted to consult a doctor there."

Christina sat down hard on the sofa. "Damn it, do I have to leave the *state* for some privacy? Who have you told?"

"No one, honey. Is the baby Grant's?"

Christina sucked on her lower lip. Oh, what the hell? What the woman didn't know, she'd guess. "Might be."

"Or could be that other hottie you were going out with—Ray Malory?" Karen gave Christina an envious look. "You are one lucky girl. Two ripe, gorgeous cowboys fighting over you. But I'm not surprised—you pull off the tank top and shorts thing well. Most women our age can't anymore."

"I won't be wearing them for much longer." The emotions tied up in that statement made Christina giddy. She'd be buying maternity clothes, baby things, planning for her new family. She wanted to burst into tears. *Damn hormones.*

"So, you're going to have the baby? Good for you. You have a lot of guts. But you still need me to drive you, or the whole town will know before you're ready for them to."

Christina considered her options — including getting on a bus and heading anywhere but here — then let out a heavy sigh.

"The appointment is at two — it's in Richardson." She and Bailey had found the clinic that could tell her not only pregnancy results right away but promised swift pre-natal results as well. And, going to Richardson instead of the clinic where everyone in town went, meant she could break the news when *she* was ready. "I'm leaving early tomorrow morning and staying overnight afterward."

"Perfect," Karen said warmly. "Gives me a chance to go to Neiman's. I need some new shoes."

***

The commercial's shoot was postponed the next day because, as Tyler said, horses happened.

Turned out that one of the geldings brought in from another ranch for training had thrush. The owner blamed the Campbells, claiming dirty conditions in their barn had led to the infection. Carter nearly went ballistic on him — their stables were always clean and dry, mucked out every day, he snapped.

Grant and Tyler had to step in and placate the owner. If Circle C's stables were the cause, Grant explained, all the other horses there would have thrush too. The Campbells would be happy to have the gelding's hooves treated for no charge.

The owner left, conceding, and Carter said the guy had just been angling for a free vet visit. But

Grant knew, and Carter agreed, that if they sent the gelding home, the owner might not bother with treatment, and the horse would suffer. Some people just shouldn't be allowed to have animals.

Then Buster, the best horse for stunt work, woke up lame, for no reason anyone could find. He limped around, not wanting to put pressure on his right foreleg. Vet was called, found nothing. Farrier called, found nothing. Buster would have to stay quiet for a couple of days, and be watched.

So much for working on the shoot—Buster was the best to ride for jumping onto trains. Grant accused him of faking it, and Buster, always bad-tempered, tried to bite him.

"If he's not better in a couple days, we'll have to use Bobby," Grant told Tyler, who reluctantly agreed.

Grant also heard through the Riverbend grapevine that Christina had driven out of town to Dallas with Karen.

Seriously crazy.

Grant went to Christina's house late in the evening to see if Christina had got back all right, but Mrs. Kaye next door told him she and Karen were staying in Dallas overnight. Didn't Grant know that?

No, Grant hadn't known. He thanked Mrs. Kaye politely and left.

He didn't like this. Why Christina had taken *Karen*, of all people with her, was weird. Something was going on, and it badly worried him that he didn't know what. Pissed him off, too.

He suspected Christina would only shut him out if he tried to call her, but he kept his cell phone close by, for once, in case she needed to get in touch for whatever reason. If Karen didn't bring Christina back tomorrow, Grant would drive north to find her, shoot or no shoot.

He'd find her, bring her home, and tell her to stay in Riverbend. With him. Where they both belonged.

***

Driving the back highways to Dallas with Karen was a surreal experience. Also very comfortable. The BMW was cushy. Soft leather seats, climate controls, soft music. It was like floating.

Karen wanted to talk, whether Christina liked it or not.

"I fell in love with my total bastard third husband pretty hard. It was his glamour, his money—he swept me off my feet. Five years into the marriage, and I find out he had *two* other houses, each containing a mistress, one of whom had two of his kids. He didn't try to marry them, at least, but he called each his wife. Nice work if you can get it. Must have cost him a hell of a lot of money, because they both lived as high on the hog as I did, but I guess he liked the power, and fooling everyone."

"You still work with him, though, don't you?" Christina asked, mildly curious.

"I own a company with him, yes, and two other people. I've invested too much money and time to walk away from that. He can buy me out if he gets tired of me. I did pretty good out of the divorce though. Stupid man never asked for a prenup, because he thought he could string me along for the rest of my life."

"I'm sorry," Christina said. "That must have been hard, finding out. My sister had a similar thing happen. Are all men total assholes?"

Karen glanced at her and smiled. "No, and you know it. Those Campbell boys are sweethearts. I'm glad in a way that Preston happened to me, because it put my life into perspective. I'm smart, and I'm driven. Now I focus on my career and what makes *me* happy. Men, I save for fun."

"Sounds good," Christina said wistfully. "Maybe I'll try to live like that."

Karen laughed in genuine mirth. "Too late for you, honey. You are madly in love with Grant, and you know it."

Christina looked out the window at the flat plain rolling past, the stretches of ranch land, the farms in the distance. "I guess that's obvious. But I doubt it will work out, even if this is his baby. We tried being together, and we just couldn't without arguing all the time. We tried so hard for me to get pregnant, and nothing. It tore us apart. And now? If Grant isn't the father, it's going to kill him."

"And if he is the father?"

"It will be ..." Christina rested her head on the back of the seat. "So wonderful. I've wanted a baby for such a long time. It's crazy complicated, but I'm so happy I don't know what to do." She wiped tears from her eyes—things were already hard enough without her crying all the time. "But Grant and I—I don't know if we can make it, even with a baby. We're not kids anymore. The hurting is adult now."

Karen's amusement returned. "Honey, you are so totally wrong, it's unbelievable. You and Grant Campbell are still together. I've had my eye on the pair of you ever since I saw you watching him in the diner that day. If looks could kill, I'd have been minced sirloin. You two might not live in the same house anymore, but you're a couple, sweetie, trust me. You would be even if you lived in different countries. You're going to have to deal with it."

Christina's mouth popped open during this speech, the air conditioning chilling her. Then she groaned.

"You're right." Christina scrubbed her face with one hand. "I don't want you to be right, but you are. What am I going to do?"

"There's only one thing *to* do, sweetie. Hold on to him. There are some real duds in the world—men who think women are put on earth for their personal pleasure, and who cares what we think? Or want? Or need? Grant's not like that."

"No," Christina said thickly. "He's not."

"And I'll tell you something else. Men are fragile. They act all macho, and they can be physically strong sometimes, but inside, they're little boys on the playground, trying to figure out where they belong. Women scare most of them to death, so they treat us like shit to compensate. But there's a few who aren't threatened, and who truly love women, everything about them. Those are the ones you want to hang on to."

Christina thought about Grant, his sexy drawl, the way his eyes went dark when he came inside her. The politeness he stuck to, no matter what, his concern for Christina and all she did.

Christina groaned again, but more softly this time. "Why is life so complicated?"

"It's not complicated. What you do is drive over to that trailer of his, move yourself in, and stay put. If you love him so much, walk in there and start loving him." Karen drove up the ramp to the 35 and put on a burst of speed. "It's easy, honey. Don't make it harder than it has to be."

Of all the advice Christina had been given about Grant, and she'd been given a lot, this was the most direct: Grab the problem by the balls and make everything work out.

Christina straightened up. "All right, but if I do move back in with Grant, I don't want to see you hanging all over him anymore. I don't share." She gave Karen a stern look. "You get your cowboy fix somewhere else."

Karen laughed. "Honey, I don't poach. I've been poached on, and I'm not going there. But, sweetie, can you blame me? Grant is one fine man. Fortunately he has brothers. Carter has a little too much residual anger in him for me, but Tyler—I can go for some of that. Or Ross, as long as he wears his uniform. Oh, maybe both together."

Christina burst out laughing. The woman was incorrigible. But also refreshingly honest.

She went quiet again. "What do I do if the baby's Ray's?"

"You cross that bridge when you come to it. Which will be soon. There's the city."

Karen gestured at the looming skyline of Dallas, bursting up out of the flat lands like a forest of steel and glass.

In a few hours, Christina would know the truth, and what direction her life would take.

***

Grant couldn't hang around outside Christina's house waiting for her to come home the next day because Carter dragged him off to the shoot.

Good thing, because he'd make a complete fool of himself pacing on Christina's porch and peering up the street. Better to go to work like a normal person.

Sort of. Normal people didn't ride their horses next to a moving old-time train, and then jump from saddle to train car and pretend to rob the passengers.

Buster was better this morning, but none of the brothers wanted to run him in case something really was wrong with him. They used Bobby and a couple others, but Grant knew they'd be re-taking some of this.

Tyler fell twice before he finally got himself on the damn train. Then it was Grant's turn. Hampered by duster, bandanna, and double holsters with pistols, Grant galloped Bobby alongside one of the passenger cars, looking for his opening.

Bobby, unlike Buster, who would run straight until he decided to stop, liked to swing his body in the opposite direction from the jump as his rider left the saddle. Grant would have to compensate for that.

Also for the fact that his mind was not on the job. He was worried about Christina and wouldn't feel good until he knew she was home. Safe.

He knew in his heart that this would be his last chance with her. Carter was right—if Grant screwed things up this time, it would be forever.

The train hit the straight stretch of track Grant had been waiting for. Bobby was right on stride. Grant crouched, readied himself, and leapt.

The handhold slid out of his grasp. Grant's gloved hands slipped, and he opened them to let himself fall, tucking in before he hit the gravel just outside the rail. He rolled like crazy, away from the clacking metal wheels, tumbling down the little embankment to prickly weeds.

Carter came riding up, looking like a real bandit in his duster, a bandolier of bullets across his chest. "You okay?" he called.

Grant rolled to his feet and brushed the dirt and dried grass off his clothes. "Yeah, I'm fine."

Carter said nothing. He never admonished them for a fall, although he was the one who answered to the producers if they were late with their material. He simply waited for Grant to make sure he hadn't broken or sprained anything, then indicate that he was all right to go again.

The advantage of Bobby was that he'd come when called, so precious time wasn't wasted chasing down a horse. Bobby had good manners, but even so, he didn't have the edge Buster did. Buster always got the job done. *Then* he ran off and was a total shit.

Grant mounted, rode Bobby around a little to work off his own stiffness, then ran the horse at the train again.

This time when Grant jumped, he caught the bar he aimed for, though barely. He felt his hands slipping, but he clung on grimly, swinging his legs until he found purchase on the step.

Then he was up and tearing inside, staying in the character of a man with one thing on his mind— robbing all the sitting ducks.

No one waited in the passenger car, because they'd film the interior scenes on a different day. Today was about jumping on and off.

The small train slowed and ground to a halt. The engineer had explained he couldn't run the train constantly because the engine used a lot of fuel, and the antique needed a rest.

Grant went out to the back platform. Tyler followed him, and Carter dismounted and joined them.

They spent a few minutes simply resting, three bandits taking a break. Grant sat with his back to the door frame, one leg drawn up, arm on his knee. Tyler swung his legs off the back. Carter remained standing, leaning against the railing, the three of them enjoying a quiet moment of Texas springtime.

Grant's cell phone jangled. His two brothers looked at him in surprise, knowing Grant's record for losing his phone. He ignored them as a hundred terrors slammed into his head—Christina in a car wreck, in a hospital, car-jacked or robbed …

He grabbed the phone, not recognizing the number. "Yeah, who's this?"

"It's Karen. You need to get over to Christina's place. I mean right now."

"Why? Is she all right? What happened? Damn it, I *knew* I shouldn't have let her go …"

"Stop talking and take yourself over there. I couldn't stay with her—I have to meet someone in Austin."

"What happened to her? Is she hurt—?"

"Christina's fine … Well, that's not for me to say. You need to get over there. And go easy on her, Grant. This has been tough for her. Buh-bye." Karen clicked off.

"Wait a minute— *Shit*." Grant shook the phone as though that would make Karen's voice come back.

Carter eyed him narrowly. "What's wrong?"

"I gotta go."

"Christina okay?" Tyler asked, concerned.

"I don't know. I need to go find out."

Grant whistled through his fingers for Bobby, who raised his head and then half walked, half trotted over.

Grant leapt from the train platform, swarmed up onto Bobby's back and rode hell for leather to the depot.

Chapter Fourteen

Grant slid off Bobby at the depot and yelled at the stable hands waiting at the horse trailers. "Walk him around, cool him down."

Without bothering to explain, he jumped into the one truck not hooked up to a trailer — Tyler's — and gunned it, sliding around in the dirt before the pickup straightened itself out.

He bumped over a mile of dirt road, then turned onto a highway, where he opened it up and roared toward town at eighty miles an hour.

He reached Christina's house, stopped the truck and leapt out, racing up to her porch. He banged on the door, but there was no answer.

Grant rattled the handle, but the door was locked. He banged again. "Christina, let me in!"

A soft step behind him made Grant swing around. Small Mrs. Kaye from next door stood on the step behind him.

"Her spare key, dear," Mrs. Kaye said, handing it to him. She looked him up and down. "My, don't you look handsome?"

Grant was still in his long duster with pistols beneath it, the bandanna loose around his neck. He'd been too distracted to take them off.

He grabbed the key. "She in there?"

"Yes, dear. Crying her eyes out."

"Shi— I mean, *shoot*. Thanks, Mrs. Kaye."

"You need to marry her," Mrs. Kaye said, giving him a serious look. "I know young people think it's old-fashioned, but a commitment like that can keep you strong, even when things look very dark. Mr. Kaye and I were married sixty years, and we were as much in love the day he died as the day he proposed." Her brown eyes shone with tears.

"Yeah," Grant said quietly. "I think you're right."

He took a breath, unlocked the door, and strode inside.

"I know I am, dear," he heard Mrs. Kaye say before the lady closed the door for him and left them alone.

***

Christina heard Grant let himself inside—locking the door and not answering didn't send a clear enough message, she guessed.

"Christina!" His deep voice boomed through the house.

Christina, sitting on the edge of her bed, didn't answer.

Grant charged through the living room and straight into the bedroom. He halted on the doorstep, all delectable six-foot four of him, made more delectable by his movie clothes. His black shirt and butt-hugging jeans emphasized his athletic body, and the worn duster and revolvers gave him a dangerous air.

When Grant saw her, he softened his abrupt tone. "Baby, what is it?"

Christina couldn't tell him. She could barely accept it herself. To be lifted up in such great hope, only to be dashed to the ground, hurt worse than any pain she'd ever experienced in her life.

She knew, though, that telling Grant she didn't want to talk about it would only make him stay and stubbornly try to pry it out of her.

She opted for straight truth.

"It was a false alarm," she said in a quiet voice. "I'm not pregnant."

Grant went motionless for a few heartbeats. His hat, which he must have automatically taken off when he walked into the house, hung at his side.

"What do you mean, you're *not* pregnant?" he asked. "Did you think you were?"

Christina nodded. She felt the tears come, tried to stop them, and gave up. "That's why I went to Dallas. I didn't want anyone knowing until I was sure."

She'd been stunned when the doctor had called her back in. "Home tests are sometimes inaccurate," the woman had said, "which is why it's good to verify the results. But you're not pregnant."

She'd said it as though Christina should be relieved.

The doctor hadn't known—Christina hadn't confided in her—that her dream of having a child had just been ripped away from her once more. Maybe for the last time.

Grant was staring at her. Christina wiped her eyes. "I was so scared about telling you I didn't know whether it was your baby or Ray's, but now ... it doesn't matter."

"Fuck," he said.

Christina swallowed. "I guess it wasn't meant to be."

She waited for him to start yelling. *What do you mean, my baby or Ray's?*

Grant dropped his hat to the bed and sat down next to her. He smelled good—dusty, full of sunshine and warmth.

"Sugar, I'm so sorry."

Grant's voice was hushed, all anger gone. Christina glanced at him and saw tears sparkling in his eyes, rendering them the deepest lake blue.

"I'm sorry too," she said. "I was so worried about how to break it to you. Even when I found out it wasn't going to happen ... I still couldn't decide whether to tell you ..."

"Karen called me and told me to come." Grant slid his arm around her shoulder. "I'm glad she did."

Christina gave him a wry smile. "I never thought Karen would be the one to hold my hand when I got the bad news."

Grant's arm tightened around her, and Christina sank into him. He was so strong, his strength comforting, no matter what the ordeal.

She thought over what Karen had said about men being fragile. She supposed Grant could be fragile—for all his strength. He'd nearly fallen apart when they'd broken up, after month after month of hoping a child would come and finally giving up. They'd both been a wreck for a long time.

Even now, Grant had just heard he'd yet again lost the chance to be a father. But he said nothing, only held her.

"I wanted this to be real," Christina said softly. "For you and me both. I wanted it so bad. When I got into the car after the appointment, I couldn't stop crying. Poor Karen."

Karen stopped at a convenience store to buy her a box of tissues. But she'd been sympathetic.

"Baby, why didn't you tell me?" Grant's voice was quiet. "I'd have gone with you. You shouldn't have had to face that alone."

"Then neither of us would have been able to drive home." Christina gave him a shaky smile. "I didn't want to tell you until I was sure. I didn't want to get your hopes up."

"Yeah, they would have been." Grant rubbed her arm. "Ray, huh?"

Christina nodded. "It was the week before the wedding, when he was going off for the rodeo. And then you and me ..."

"Lost it in my trailer. I remember." Grant blew out his breath. "Hell, yeah, do I remember."

"I was so happy. Scared, but happy. And then ..."

Christina had been crying since she'd come home. She'd tried to stop—the distraction of Grant storming in had helped a little, but the tears wouldn't dry up.

The sobs returned. Poured out. She ended up with her head on Grant's chest, his arms around her. He kissed her hair, said "Shh, sweetheart."

Grant smelled of horse, leather, smoke from the train, himself. He held her securely in his arms, protecting her from the world once again. Christina put her arms around him and hung on.

Not long later, they were lying on top of the bed, Grant's caresses gentle. Both were fully clothed — Grant in his Wild West gear, minus his prop guns, Christina in her tank top and denim shorts.

It hurt so much. The thought of at last carrying a baby had twined around her heart, bathing her in elation.

Losing that hope was one of the hardest things she'd ever had to go through.

Grant kissed her gently, touched her face, her throat. His eyes were red-rimmed and full of tears, and broke her heart.

They held each other for a long, long time, lying full length, saying nothing, using touches and little kisses to let the other know they were there. The sun sank, slanting warmth through the bedroom windows.

After a while, Christina said, "Your shoot. Did I mess it up for you?"

The bed moved with his shrug. "Doesn't matter. Buster was out, anyway. But hell, baby, even if everything had been perfect, I'd have come."

"Carter will probably rip you a new one," Christina said, trying to find humor. But she felt limp, spent, as though she'd never laugh again.

"Carter can suck on it. But he'd understand if he knew why."

Christina flattened her hand against his chest. "Please, don't tell anyone. I don't want to have to explain."

"You know I won't, sweetheart."

"And not Ray. Please. Even with this, I wasn't thinking about going back to him. It's over for good. I meant that."

Grant's eyes flickered. "I might still kill him. I just won't tell him why."

"Leave it, Grant. Please?"

"Don't worry, love. I won't talk to Ray. Don't really want to."

"I'm sorry." Christina sighed. "And I'm so tired of saying sorry."

"Then quit doing it. I believe you about Ray. I don't want to go buy him flowers and tell him he and I should love each other, but I know you two are done. We need to move on."

"Move on to what?" Christina asked, sad.

"I don't know." Grant caressed her cheek, letting his fingers trail to her shoulder. "All I know is I don't want you moving out of Riverbend. Not yet. Not until I find out if we have a chance together."

Christina didn't want to leave either. She loved Riverbend, in spite of how much she complained, and she knew it.

"I made a big show of quitting my job," she said dolefully. "I'd need it back if I stayed. I have a little put aside, but it won't last forever. Bailey and I are buying this house together—I need to keep up my half. Plus there's food, electricity—you know, all those luxuries."

"Christina, I have money. And you know I've always wanted to take care of you."

A gorgeous cowboy looking at her with those blue eyes and telling her that was hard to resist.

Christina had to smile. "I remember fighting about that too. I like to pay my own way, and you know it. I'm not going to be the lady who lunches and has an affair with the tennis pro because her rich husband is too busy for her."

Grant gave her a patient look. "Sweetie, this is Riverbend, not Beverley Hills. We don't have tennis pros."

She flicked her fingers against his chest. "You know what I mean. I want to contribute—we should be partners, not me being the cook and housekeeper while you take honeys out to lunch."

"Hey, did I ever say we'd be like that?"

"No," Christina said with a straight face. "You're a total feminist, not a macho bone in you."

Grant's eyes widened. "I wouldn't go *that* far."

Lying on her bed, in his black clothes and duster, looking like he'd just robbed a train and ridden home to his woman, Grant was more macho than this feminine room could take. The lacy pillows didn't stand a chance. He was getting them very dirty. Bailey wouldn't be happy.

No, Bailey would understand. She'd married a Campbell.

"I mean I don't want you to buy me," Christina said. She loosened the bandanna around his neck. The top buttons of his shirt were undone, showing a sliver of liquid-dark skin.

"Okay, I won't give you a penny. You can sleep in the basement and eat crusts of bread, and I'll eat off gold plates upstairs."

"In your trailer." Christina touched the hollow of his throat. "Yeah, that would work."

"Fine—you go work and earn a ton of cash, and then I'll stay home and drink beer. Sounds fair to me."

"You'd get fat and slobby." Christina poked his stomach, which was rock-hard. "Then I'd have to go find that tennis pro. I like a man who can move."

"Oh, I can move, sweetheart."

Grant swiftly pushed her into the bed, coming over her to cover her mouth with a long kiss. He slid hands down her body as he kissed her, but quietly, soothing. Warming her.

Christina held on to him and lost herself in the kiss. She tasted his tears and his grief, felt his body tight with emotion.

She loved him so much. Even when they'd fought all during the years, Christina had loved Grant with everything she had.

They went on kissing, and when the kiss drew to its end, they simply touched, gliding fingers over each other's bodies. Sometimes they kept to the fabric, sometimes they dipped beneath their clothes to brush bare skin.

They seemed to have a tacit agreement to not take it to full sex. They needed comfort right now, to simply be in each other's company. The frenzy of love-making would come later.

The sun sank, bathing them in darkness. Only then did Grant rise from the bed and skim off his clothes. He slowly stripped Christina, dropping her shirt, shorts, and panties to the floor, and then lay down with her again.

Grant slid inside her without haste. Christina was slick, wanting him, a groan leaving her mouth as he spread and filled her.

The feeling of Grant inside her was so right. He belonged with her. Their hearts and bodies understood—their heads were what needed to catch up.

Grant went slowly at first, Christina running her hands over his taut, wonderful body, finding every hollow of him. She pressed his hips as they rose and fell, and under her touch, he went faster, then faster still.

The fever didn't hit until the end, when they were grappling, crying out, sliding against each other. Grant groaned, *"Damn,"* at the same time Christina was lifted by intense joy, the two of them coming against each other.

Then breathlessness, quiet kissing, winding down.

Grant slept, his head pillowed on Christina's shoulder. She contemplated his closed eyes, lashes black against his skin, his bed-mussed hair, the curve of shoulder, the rise and fall of his chest. Relaxed, worn out, but with a little pucker between his brows that wouldn't smooth away.

Christina's tears dropped to Grant's cheek and rolled down to be lost in shadows.

***

Grant woke as twilight was settling in and got up to take a shower, pulling the sheet over Christina's naked body. She kept sleeping—worn out, the little sweetheart.

In Christina's very clean bathroom, Grant washed away the day and their lovemaking and re-dressed in his jeans and shirt.

Grants emotions had been shot high and slammed back down. Worry for Christina, heartache when she explained about the false hope of a baby after they tried so hard, anger when she said Ray might be the father, and then grief over the whole situation. Then, at the end of it all, making love to the woman he wanted to be with.

If Grant and Christina had been able to conceive during their relationship, would they have married and even now be settled down and happy? Maybe living in a little house like this, taking the kids to school and church, teaching them to ride?

Or would they have fought as much and broken up anyway? Who knew?

Grant put that speculation aside. He couldn't live by what might have been; he had to deal with what was.

He loved Christina, and he wanted to be with her. That was a certainty.

When they'd made love in the trailer, they'd talked about taking their relationship all the way back to the beginning—Grant asking Christina out on a date. He'd figure out how to do that, and make her see they had to try.

Christina was one stubborn female, who could piss Grant off quicker than anybody. But then, if she were busy pissing him off, that meant she was with him. And once they both got over being mad, Grant and Christina could make up.

Wasn't the making up worth the fight in the first place?

Christina was still asleep when Grant left. He didn't wake her—she needed the rest. He'd start wooing her when she felt better. He went out into the fine Texas evening, the temperature just right, the crickets starting to sing.

Mrs. Kaye popped out from the shadows of her rosebushes as Grant stepped off the porch. He suppressed his yell of surprise and landed back on earth.

"Mrs. Kaye," he said, breathless.

"Did you ask her to marry you?" Mrs. Kaye asked, glancing at the closed door.

"Not yet." Grant sent her a grin. "But I'm working on it."

"You keep trying. You two belong together."

Grant settled his hat on his head. "I agree with you, ma'am. Have a good night."

He nodded at her and turned back to Tyler's truck. Tyler had probably shit a brick when he realized Grant had taken it. *All in a good cause, bro.*

At the Circle C Ranch Grant walked into the kitchen, hungry as hell. A woman stood at the stove with his back to him.

"I kept you something warm," she said. "Faith's already had her dinner. You work too hard, your mom says. Maybe ... I don't know ... we could go out and have a beer?"

"I just came in," Grant said.

Grace Malory spun around, eyes wide, and her face went an interesting shade of bright red. "Oh, crap. It's you."

"Yep." Grant dumped his long coat on a chair, his prop pistols on the table, then yanked open the refrigerator and came out with a cold bottle of beer. "Who'd you think it was?" He snapped his fingers as though he'd just figured it out. "Carter, right?"

Chapter Fifteen

"Grant Campbell, don't you ever, ever tell a soul I just did that." Grace's voice was fierce, her hands clenching a dishtowel.

Grant's mood lifted the slightest bit. "You mean don't tell anyone that you asked Carter on a date when he wasn't even in the room? Or were you just shooting for a Campbell brother, any brother?"

"Quit making fun of me. This is embarrassing."

Grant took a sip of beer, enjoying the cold on his dry throat. "Good thing it *was* me that came in. I bet Carter would have just grunted and made an excuse."

Her face fell. "You think so? I was hoping he might like me a little — as a friend if nothing else."

"He does like you. But I gotta warn you that Carter's hard on his friends. He doesn't have any female ones at all. His look on women is slightly ... skewed."

Grace relaxed her hold on the towel. "Because of Faith's mom?"

"Partly. Carter went through a lot of hardship before he came here, most of which he won't talk about." Grant gentled his tone. "Be careful you don't hurt yourself on him."

Grace sighed. "It's stupid, I know. But he's just ... just so ..."

"If you say *dreamy*, I'm going to pour this beer all over you."

"Shut up." Grace softened the words. "Guess I'm glad you saved me from making a big fool of myself."

Grant glanced around the kitchen. There were pots in the sink and plates of food covered with foil on the counter. Everything smelled good, and his stomach growled.

"What are you doing here, anyway?" he asked. "Another bake sale?"

Grace moved to the stove and stirred something in a pot. "I came by to bring your mom a recipe, and I found her going crazy trying to run things down at the stables and cook for you all. She was yelling about not having enough time to make dinner for the menfolk—her word—and high-tailed it back to the stables again. So I thought I'd save her some trouble and put together some supper for whoever came in."

Grant was impressed. "That was nice of you."

"Not really. I'm bored out of my mind, so helping her out is helping *me* out."

Grant took a peek at what was being kept warm on the plates—roast beef, some baked potatoes, rolls, veg ... "This all looks pretty good."

"Just a little something."

Right. A four-course meal plus what smelled like pie in the oven was a *little something*.

"Tell you what." Grant reverently lowered the foil on a plate. "My mom could use help around here, and you're one hell of a cook. Why don't you work for her? You'd get paid and have something to do, Mom could relax, and Faith would have square meals, not to mention the rest of us."

"Work here?" Grace stared at him, her flush returning. "Like, every day?"

"I bet Mom would give you a day off every once in a while. How about it? You'd have more chances of catching Carter's eye if you were right under his nose."

Grace's flush deepened. "Is it that obvious?" Then she sighed. "Oh, what the hell? But ask Olivia first before you sign me up. She might not like the idea."

"She will," Grant said. He slid back the foil on another plate and plucked up a few tidbits of meat. "She likes to eat as much as any of us. Let me talk to her, and I'll fix it up."

Grace beamed. "Thanks, Grant. You're a good person." She grasped his sleeve and rose on tiptoe to kiss his cheek.

Carter chose that moment to walk in. Grant didn't miss the flash of anger in his brother's eyes as Grant took a nonchalant sip of beer. Grace wiped her hands, waved Carter at the food, then grabbed her purse and scurried out the back door.

Carter's fury with Grant *might* have been because Grant had left an important shoot earlier today, but he didn't think so. Grant would bet good money that it was all about the kiss.

***

Christina decided to swallow her pride and tell her uncle she'd go back to work for him. She'd made the decision to stay in Riverbend, but she hadn't been kidding when she said she didn't want to be Grant's kept woman. She'd have her own job, stand on her own two feet, as she always had, whether she and Grant could make it together again or not. Her uncle was delighted she'd decided to stay, and told her she could start any time; all she had to do was talk to the manager and work out a schedule.

Christina put off starting again until she finished moving out of her old apartment and set up Bailey's house. She then took her time settling in, telling herself she didn't need the income yet.

She knew she was taking the time to get over the disappointment of not being pregnant, the wound of that still raw. Grant did talk to her, calling her to make sure she was all right, but Christina put off seeing him as well. She needed to heal before tackling life again.

She was happy she hadn't run around telling everyone her exciting news, because she'd have had to swallow that now and take their sympathy, which she wouldn't have been able to stand. Grant also said nothing to anyone, and neither did Karen, though Karen checked up on Christina from time to time. Their expedition and conversations had formed into a friendship, even if it was the oddest friendship Christina had ever had.

Finally, one evening a few weeks later, Christina made herself go to the bar and talk to the manager. She didn't really want to go out, but then again, she didn't want to mope in her house either. Christina needed to keep moving, even if right now she was shattered.

Christina walked the short distance to the tavern in the cool dark air, waving to her friends as she entered. She started for the back office, but Karen intercepted her and pulled her aside.

"Are you doing all right?" Karen asked her, bending close so no one else would hear. They stood in a corner near the end of the counter, Karen's business suit today a cream linen skirt, blue silk blouse, and black jacket. Christina always felt underdressed next to her, though tonight she'd worn the cutest spaghetti strap top she owned and denim shorts. *Most women our age can't pull that off anymore, my ass.*

Christina nodded in answer to Karen's question. She was doing fine physically, but she knew what Karen meant. "I'll be okay."

Karen gave her a look that said she didn't really believe Christina, but she wouldn't pry. For some reason that was easier to take than an outburst of sympathy and hugs.

"I hear you want to work here again," Karen said. "Your uncle told me. I told *him* that I don't want you tending bar here anymore."

Christina looked at her in astonishment. "What? Why not? Do you already own the place? When did this happen?"

"It wasn't official until late this afternoon. A few formalities and the deal is closed." Karen studied Christina with a serious look. "I don't want you bartending, because I want you in the back office, running the place for me."

Christina started. "Running it? My uncle runs it ...."

"Your uncle wants to retire. He deserves time to relax." Karen rested her elbow on the back of a tall chair. "Don't worry, I'm not trying to run an elderly man out of town on a rail. Sam told me when I talked to him this evening that he wants to call it quits. He also suggested that you would be the best person for the job. You know everyone in town, you can work with the suppliers, and he says you're more trustworthy than anyone else. I think he's right."

Run the place, work in the office, be the boss. Be responsible for everything. Scary, and at the same time, intriguing. Christina perked up for the first time since her trip to the clinic.

"I'm interested," Christina said. "Salary?"

Karen gave her a smile. "I think I can make you an offer you'll like."

"In that case, sure, let's talk."

"It's not the most glamorous job in the world," Karen said warningly. "But it will give you good experience, help you grow—who knows, maybe open your own establishment someday. You've stayed doing one thing for so long, trying to be the perfect girlfriend for Grant, that you've neglected to be the perfect person for yourself." The problem with Karen was that her observations tended to be exactly on target.

"Don't start tonight," Karen said. "Sit down, relax, and enjoy yourself. Observe the bar from this side of things. You deserve a break."

Well, Christina could stand to try to take her mind off things. She was still upset, and she knew she would be for a very long time, but she did have friends here, people she loved and who loved her. She needed a few minutes of comfort.

She asked Rosie to make her a virgin strawberry daiquiri, and even that innocuous request brought her pain. When the home pregnancy test had been positive, Christina had been relieved that she wasn't a drinker. Not only had working in a bar made her not want to drink often, but when she and Grant had started trying for a baby, she'd given it up altogether. Just in case.

Christina stuck with abstaining, even through the disappointments, and she stuck to it now. And even that was a reminder of pain.

Then again, she needed to stop being maudlin and get on with things. She needed to learn to deal with it.

She took the daiquiri to an empty table and sat down to try to enjoy the slushy, fruity drink.

It was dance night at the bar. A local band played the latest tunes mixed with classics plus some originals they were working on. The cleared floor filled with couples two-stepping or just moving to the music.

"Drinking alone, little lady?" A tall body filled her vision, and Grant sank into the empty place at her table. "Mind if a cowboy pulls up a chair?"

Christina met his blue gaze, which was quiet, shuttered. She hadn't seen Grant since he'd left her house the night she'd returned from Dallas, and she'd been grateful to him for not pushing her. She needed time. Grant had called her every day, and they'd talked, but they'd kept their conversations easy, free of drama. Christina appreciated that.

"If you want," she said, waving her hand at him. "It's a free country."

Grant gave her a nod. "I saw a pretty lady sitting here, and I thought—I need to get to know her. Hi, I'm Grant." He stuck out his hand.

Christina's heart beat faster as she put her hand into his warm, strong grip. "I'm Christina."

"Pretty name for a pretty lady. Want to dance?"

"I don't know. I'm happy sipping my drink."

"Well, okay, sipping's good too."

Grant, who'd kept the handshake lingering, finally released her—slowly—then signaled to the waitress. The woman, who'd worked there for years, said, "Hey, Grant. Let me guess—draft beer?" and headed back to the bar.

"Do you come here a lot?" Christina asked, poking at her pink drink with the skinny straws.

"Grew up in Riverbend." Grant folded his arms on the table, his T-shirt with *Circle C Ranch* on it stretching over his chest. "Have a ranch not too far down the road. My family does, that is. We own it together."

"That sounds nice."

The beer landed on the table. The waitress winked at Christina then turned away.

Grant picked up the foaming mug and took a preliminary sip. "What do you do?"

"Well, starting now, I run this bar. The whole thing." Christina made a sweeping gesture that took in the room.

Grant blinked and dropped the pretense. "You do?"

"Yep. Karen made me an offer I couldn't refuse."

Grant's brows went up. "Karen, the woman you vowed you'd never, ever work for? At the top of your lungs?"

Christina flushed. "Yes, okay. Turns out, she's not so bad."

Grant chuckled, and the sound did things to Christina's heart. "It took me a while to warm up to her too." He glanced at the crowd. "Come and dance with me. I want my arms around you."

Now *that* was a good pick-up line. Christina rose to her feet. "Sure."

Grant flashed his warm smile and led her out to the dance floor.

Christina never got tired of being held by his strong body. Grant spun her around with the athleticism that showed when he rode, his steps sure. He never let her get out of sync with the music.

Christina floated on a cushion of sound, steadied by Grant's arms. She loved that cowboys could work hard all day and then put on clean clothes and dance the night away.

Everyone in town seemed to be here tonight, dancing, forgetting cares, enjoying themselves.

Grant pulled Christina a step closer, leaned down, and kissed her.

A slow, warm, loving kiss. Christina felt her heart lighten, her devastation about her visit to Dallas easing for a brief moment. Grant was here, and they might have another chance.

She let him walk her home. Christina debated whether she should end the "date" with a simple good night or invite him in for a wonderful evening's natural conclusion.

When Grant kissed her under the porch light, Christina wrapped her hands around the lapels of his shirt and pulled him inside.

***

Grant's hopes were high as he lay with Christina that night, their bodies together in the darkness. This was the way it used to be, the two of them making love, then talking together, then kissing in quietude, then making love again.

Grant was still in her bed when the sun came up, touching them both with warmth. They rolled out of bed at the same time, covered their nakedness with what they could grab, and went out to make breakfast in the kitchen.

Like old times. How easily they fell back into the routine.

"Come to the shoot with me," Grant said as he poured himself another cup of coffee. Christina was sexy as hell in a short robe over nothing at all, backless slippers on her feet. "We're doing the interior shots today. And maybe jumping from the moving cars, if we have time. You can watch me try not to break my neck."

Christina hesitated. Grant took another sip of coffee, waiting for her to say no.

She'd explain that they were taking things too fast, she wasn't ready, all the many things women liked to say when they wanted a man to go away. *Don't let the screen door hit you.*

Then Christina nodded. "Sounds fun. I'm not meeting with Karen about the job until this evening. I have the day free."

The relief Grant felt surprised him. He hid it with another sip of his thick black coffee.

She didn't have to worry, Grant thought. He wasn't about to push them into moving in together, marrying, settling down. Not yet. He'd give her time to heal, to get used to the idea. But he wasn't going to let it go either.

Christina taking the job at the bar meant she was staying in Riverbend. They'd have time to become comfortable with each other again. No pushing.

They'd broken up last time from all the pushing. Maybe they were older now, and wiser.

Not so old Grant couldn't get hard watching Christina swish around the kitchen in that thin little yellow robe. Not long later, she was straddling him in a kitchen chair, while the room rang with their cries of passion and the bacon burned.

They were late to the shoot, but Carter's annoyed look turned to understanding when he saw Christina get out of the truck with Grant.

"She's going to be an extra in the robbery scene," Grant explained.

Carter gave Christina a nod. "Good. We need more women. Costuming is in the depot."

"Good morning to you too, Carter." Christina caught his elbow and kissed his cheek then waltzed off to the depot.

Carter said nothing, but he looked pleased.

***

It was fun—for a while—pretending to be a train passenger from a hundred and thirty years ago, getting robbed by Wild West bandits.

Especially when one of the bandits was Grant. Christina, sitting in the rather hard train seat in her high-necked, long-skirted dress, fantasized about the train robber with the beautiful blue eyes, who'd sweep her up and carry her off to ravish her privately.

Hard to act terrified of the gunslinger when Christina had woken up with him this morning, sunlight brushing his bronze-colored skin. Grant's touch on her had been gentle, caressing the marks his mouth had left on her last night.

After the small train went around on its circular tracks about ten times, however, and they did the scene again and again, the fun started to ebb.

Christina was getting motion sick on the swaying, stuffy car. By the time the extras were finally released, she was hot, sweating, and ready to hurl.

Changing back to her regular clothes then sitting outside at the depot to watch the stunt work helped some. There was a breeze, and the early April day was pleasantly cool.

The train went around again. Grant came flying off the back, landed, rolled, grabbed his running horse and swung onto the saddle, galloping off into the grasses.

Tyler and Carter each did their jumps from the train, Tyler making his leap to his horse by putting his hands on the horse's backside and vaulting forward into the saddle.

Next they did a shot of all of them jumping off at the same time, only they didn't bother getting on the horses for that one. Every piece of action would be cobbled together later by the editors to produce a smooth sequence of events.

The director wanted more shots, but it was getting late and Carter stopped him.

"Don't want to wear out the horses," he said. "We've done enough for the day."

Christina was happy to head out to the parking lot to watch Grant help his brothers load the horses into trailers. They'd used Buster today, and he didn't want to go back into his trailer. Finally Grant coaxed him in with Carter and Tyler blocking from behind, and the trailer door shut. Buster kicked it once, just to be a shit, then settled down.

Grant came back to Christina, half exasperated, half amused by Buster's antics, and gave her a kiss good-bye. He had to return to the ranch with Carter and Tyler to look after the horses, but Christina was grateful to go home alone to rest. Acting was a lot of work, she reflected. There was a lot of sitting around waiting, and then going over the same scene again and again. Exhausting.

Christina was so worn out and overheated that she called Karen and canceled the meeting for tonight. Karen didn't sound happy but rescheduled for the next evening. They'd have dinner, she said, six o'clock, at Mrs. Ward's diner. From Karen's tone, Christina knew she'd better show up.

Grant called from the ranch's office, using the land line because he'd lost his cell phone again.

"Want some dinner?" he asked.

Hearing his velvet tones made Christina's blood warm, but she knew she couldn't get up from where she lay on the bed even for Grant tonight. And the thought of food made her even queasier. "I feel like crap, to be honest," she said. "Throwing up on you would embarrass the hell out of me, so I'm just going to have some club soda or something and go to sleep. Your own fault, making me train sick."

"You okay?" Grant's concern warmed her even more.

"I'll be fine. Just need some sleep. No more going around in circles for five hours again, all right?"

"You got it, sweetheart. But hey, you know, it's a paycheck." Karen's production company paid their extras. A lot of smaller studios didn't.

"Looking forward to it," Christina said sincerely.

"You call me if you need anything, all right?" Grant said. "I'll try to find my phone, but don't hesitate to call Carter or my mom. They'll get me."

Grant let her go after a few minutes of whispered sexy talk, like they used to do. Finally he said, "Good night, baby. Remember, call me if you need me."

"You got it. Good night." Christina wanted to add, but wasn't sure she should, *Love you.*

She felt better when she hung up. She'd missed every nuance of their life together.

In the morning, Christina barely made it to the bathroom before she lost the contents of her stomach. She felt better after that, but still shaky, so she called her doctor and made an appointment to see her that afternoon.

"I might have the flu," Christina said as she sat on the end of the exam table. "Or heatstroke."

She should have asked for a break yesterday. It had been too hot, she wasn't used to the heavy costumes, and the other extras had been flagging too. But they'd all stubbornly kept on, wanting to show how tough they were, Christina thought. Besides, getting frisked by Grant over and over again hadn't been a bad thing.

Her doctor worked at the clinic at the crossroads, the same one Christina had brought Ray to when they'd been in a car accident last fall. Everyone in River County came to this clinic.

Dr. Sue, a fifty-something woman with short blond hair, three kids, and a husband who was a pediatrician, studied the file a nurse had walked in to give her, then put her hand on Christina's bare knee.

"You don't have the flu, Christina," she said. "You're pregnant, sweetie."

Chapter Sixteen

Christina gaped, the dizziness she'd finally managed to shake swamping her again. "No, I can't be."

"Did you have sex with a man?" Dr. Sue asked, her look impish. "That's how women get pregnant, Christina. I remember telling you that when you were sixteen."

"Well yes, but I mean ..." Christina struggled to think. "I went to a doctor in Dallas. She said I wasn't pregnant. I'd thought I was ..." She rapidly explained.

Dr. Sue listened without changing expression. "Let me see if I've got this right. You went to a clinic, where there were about forty women in the waiting room, and the lab there ran a quick test. No chance of getting the sample mixed up, or the wrong thing written down on the wrong record?"

Christina clutched the end of the table. "I couldn't come *here*, because you know it would have been all

over town, people speculating on why I went to my
doctor this week when my yearly checkup is always
in June."

"I do understand, Christina, but if you'd come to
me, you'd have gotten the correct results, and saved
yourself a trip and a lot of money. I had the lab
downstairs look for pregnancy as well as other
things. When a healthy young woman who is
obviously back with her boyfriend suddenly doesn't
feel well, I guess pregnancy, and I'm usually right."

Christina still couldn't breathe. "Do you mean
you think I was really pregnant when I went to
Dallas? This isn't something that happened last
week?"

Dr. Sue shook her head. "Based on when you
missed your period and all my experience ..." Dr.
Sue rested her hand briefly on Christina's abdomen.
"I'd say you were about six or seven weeks gone."

Another wave of dizziness hit her. When Dr. Sue
moved her hand, Christina laid her own on her
lower abdomen. Could she feel...?

Dr. Sue gave her a smile. "I'd talk to Grant.
Congratulations, Christina. This is so wonderful."

Christina gnawed her lower lip. "If I've been
pregnant seven weeks, then there's a problem."

"Ah," Dr. Sue said, though her bright look didn't
fade. "There's a chance the baby is Ray Malory's."

Christina nodded, her face hot.

"Fortunately, there's a way to find out who the
father is without risking the baby," Dr. Sue said.
"Because we certainly don't want any risks. I'm
going to make sure you have this baby and it's
healthy and so are you. Don't worry about that. We
can do a test of your blood—they can isolate the

baby's DNA in your bloodstream, but we'll have to wait until you're at least nine weeks along. And we'd need a DNA sample from both men for comparison, of course."

"Oh." Christina had hoped that there would be a high tech test they could do today to rule out one man or the other.

Dr. Sue gave her a wise look. "It means you have to sit them down and tell them. They're both good men, raised well. I'm sure they'll consent to giving a sample."

Christina was certain they would as well. That wasn't the problem.

The problem was explaining the situation, finding out how Grant and Ray took the news, and deciding what was best for the kid.

I'm putting my baby's welfare first. Always.

This was terrifying. And so effing wonderful. Christina's doldrums of the last weeks evaporated in one second. Here was the relief the doctor in Dallas expected her to feel, except for the opposite reason.

Karen had told Christina she'd put other people ahead of herself for too long, and Christina agreed, to a point. But this changed everything.

"Oh, my God, I'm pregnant." Christina beamed a huge smile at Dr. Sue, then she started to cry. "I'm actually pregnant. Thank you, God. Thank you."

"Yes, you are," Dr. Sue said. "I was wondering when it would hit you."

***

Christina planned to tell Grant first, but Bailey called Christina as she was climbing into her truck for the drive home. Bailey and Adam were heading back to Riverbend during a break in shooting—they were both homesick and ready to slow down for a few days.

Christina couldn't stop herself blurting out the news.

Bailey was silent on the other end of the line for a long time. Then she shrieked. "So it's true after all!" she yelled with both laughter and tears in her voice. "Grant?"

"I don't know." Christina told Bailey all Dr. Sue had said. Both of them cried and laughed, then cried again.

"What am I going to do?" Christina wailed. Her emotions were flying high. She'd have to take some deep breaths before she drove.

"Nothing," Bailey said. "You wait until I'm there tomorrow. I'll take care of everything."

***

Grant still had a hell of a lot of work to do on the commercial, so he didn't have a chance to meet up with Christina the morning after her train shots. He called her, worried about her being sick, but she told him she was fine, just busy, like he was.

He let her go, but he planned to go over to her house when he finished up for the day, and make sure she was all right. If she still felt bad, he'd convince her to stay home for the night—with him— so he could take care of her.

Before that happened, Bailey and Adam returned.

"What the hell?" Grant said as he strode out of the office in the late afternoon light, still in his shoot attire. "Why didn't you two tell us you were coming?"

"We wanted to surprise you," Bailey said. She kissed Grant on the cheek, then went off to greet the rest of the household.

Grant was very glad to see his older brother, missing him more than he wanted to admit. Adam had always been the brother Grant confided in when he could talk to no one else.

Adam looked better. When he'd come home last fall, he'd been badly burned from an accident during a movie stunt. He'd healed physically pretty quickly, but the scars remained, inside and out.

Bailey had helped him through, and though Adam wasn't one hundred percent better, he'd vastly improved. Bailey was working some kind of magic.

Faith squealed and squealed when she saw Bailey, and Bailey spent a long time hugging her. The two had become very close when Bailey had worked at the ranch last year. Then Bailey took off to see Christina—good, Grant didn't like Christina being alone—leaving Grant and Adam together on the porch.

Adam talked a while about his new movie in California, but finally he broke off and simply looked at Grant. "You're way too quiet. What's going on?"

"A lot of shit," Grant said.

He told the whole story of events since Adam had gone—Karen's arrival, Christina lurking in Grant's bedroom and how they'd not been able to keep their hands off each other, Grant's hope that his reconnection with Christina could be permanent.

He omitted the part about Christina thinking she was pregnant and discovering otherwise. That was too personal and tender, plus Grant had promised he'd keep his mouth shut.

"Sounds like you two are at a crossroads." Adam rolled his cold bottle of beer around in his hands. "Do you walk on together, or take separate paths?"

Grant growled. "When did you get so damn philosophical?"

Adam's grin pulled at the scars on the left side of his face. "When I surrendered to the fall and let myself hit the landing pad that was Bailey."

"Now you're talking like a bad movie script."

"I don't see the problem with Christina," Adam said. "Sounds to me like you got to grab hold of her and hang on. Make her see that the two of you are better together than you'll ever be on your own."

Grant took a sip of beer. "That easy?"

"Yep. That's all there is to it."

"Huh. Like you didn't have to be smacked upside the head to see that Bailey was the one for you."

"Yeah, well." Adam shrugged. "I got there in the end."

They drank in silence for a time, two brothers who didn't need to talk to each other to be understood.

"I see y'all have everything under control here at the ranch," Adam said after a while. "More or less. I noticed that when Grace is cooking in the kitchen, Carter won't come in the house."

"Faith really likes her," Grant said. "And I like Grace's chicken-fried steak. That is some good stuff."

"I'm looking forward to trying it," Adam said.

"Now that you are home," Grant said after another stretch of companionable silence. "I've got a business proposition for you. It might not make us any money, but then again, we might be surprised."

"Yeah?" Adam looked interested. "Tell me."

Grant did. Adam's smile grew to an all-out grin as they talked. "Let's do it," Adam said when Grant finished. "Sounds like fun."

"I'll drink to that," Grant said. They clicked bottles.

It was good to have Adam home again.

***

The next morning, Bailey called Grant while he was getting ready to head out to the ranch, and told him to go to Christina's, where she'd spent the night, instead. Her tone was cheerful, but Bailey always sounded cheerful, even when she was delivering bad news.

Grant headed into town as quick as he could, stopped his truck outside Christina's house, and went swiftly up to the porch. Bailey opened the front door before he could knock.

Christina sat on the living room sofa, looking fine in shorts, a blouse, and sandals. She usually went barefoot in the house, so her wearing shoes, even sandals, meant something was up.

Before Grant could ask, Bailey, who'd gone back to watching out the front window, opened the door and let in Ray Malory, who paused on the threshold and gave Grant a belligerent look.

"What's going on?" Ray demanded of Grant.

"Hell if I know," Grant said. He didn't like this. "Christina?"

Bailey pointed at the two chairs on either side of the sofa. "Sit."

Grant and Ray looked at each other. Ray had come from his ranch, his boots leaving bits of dust and hay on the carpet. The fact that neither woman said anything about that didn't bode well.

Grant went to the chair on Christina's right and sat down. Ray took the other chair. Christina said nothing, only looked straight ahead, her eyes on empty space.

Bailey remained standing, putting herself opposite Christina, completing the square. It was Bailey who spoke.

"Christina went to see Dr. Sue the other day, who confirmed that Christina is pregnant. From the timing, the father could be either you, Grant, or you, Ray."

Grant's heart leapt high then started pounding hard. He surged to his feet. "But—"

"*Shh.*" Bailey jammed her finger to her lips then pointed at the chair. "Sit down. You can talk when I'm done."

Grant tried to catch Christina's eye, but she wasn't looking at anyone, not even Bailey. He clenched his hands, trying to tamp down both his elation and trepidation and sank down to the edge of the chair. Ray sat tense as a bull in a chute on the other side of the room, his breath coming fast, his gaze fixed on Christina.

Bailey continued. "Dr. Sue can run a blood test on Christina to confirm which of you is the father without doubt. All she needs is a DNA swab from each of you. Christina wanted you both to know, so you could have a fair chance at deciding what you want to do."

Grant waited a beat, in case Bailey had more to say, but she appeared to be done talking. He got to his feet again, and Ray rose with him.

"Are you sure about him?" Grant asked Christina before Ray could speak. "You weren't pregnant when you came back from Dallas, but now you are. That makes *me* the daddy, unless you decided to run off to Ray again in these last few nights."

Christina nodded. "Dr. Sue says I've been pregnant all along—the Dallas clinic was wrong. She called them, they looked it up, and admitted they wrote the wrong result on my test. They offered to redo the test, free of charge. Real sweet of them."

"Seriously?" Ray switched his glare to Grant. "*You* knew about this, but I didn't?"

Christina broke in. "When I thought it was a mistake, I saw no reason to tell you, Ray. I didn't want you to know until I was sure I was pregnant at all—and now I'm sure. From the timing, there's a very good chance you're the father."

Grant knew she believed it—feared that the baby was Ray's. She'd never have called Ray here and put him through this, or Grant either, if she hadn't been pretty damn sure.

"And that's supposed to make me feel better?" Ray snapped.

Christina bathed Ray in the same scowl she'd given Grant. "I could have waited to tell you until I knew whether or not the baby was Grant's, but I thought that wouldn't be fair to you. So I'm telling you now."

Ray subsided, but his green eyes glittered in anger. "How soon can we find out?"

"About two weeks from now. Apparently the test doesn't work before I'm nine weeks gone, and I'm about seven weeks now."

"We have to wait *two weeks*?" Ray repeated. "Shit."

Grant agreed. He felt like he'd been kicked in the stomach. Two weeks of wondering whether the kid the love of his life carried was his or not? He'd go insane.

Because Grant feared, deep in his heart, that the child was Ray's. It had to be. He and Christina had tried so hard before, and ... nothing.

Now another man was in the picture, and Christina was suddenly pregnant. It was as if all his dreams and his nightmares were coming true at the same time.

Ray was studying Christina's marble-still face. "I know you broke it off with me, Christina, because you were falling in love with Grant again. I get that. I won't try to convince you to come back to me. But if the kid is mine, I want to be its dad. I want to be in his life ... or her life. I want him to know I'm his father, and do all the dad things. All right?"

"I didn't think you'd want it otherwise," Christina said. "Grant?"

Grant could barely speak. "Hey, if the kid is Ray's, I'm not going to keep him away. But I'm not standing aside so you can marry him. I'm only so noble, Christina. Like hell I'm letting you go."

"I don't want to marry Ray," Christina said quietly.

Ray's face went redder still. "Well, thanks a lot."

"I'm sorry," she said. "But you were right. I never got over Grant. I probably never will."

The joy of that seared into Grant, the rightness of it. Christina was beautiful, inside and out, and his. "You're everything to me, sugar," he said quietly.

Ray bent a severe look on Grant. "But if Grant turns tail and runs, I'll step in and do the decent thing. If not ... I can't stop you from being with the guy you want to be with. But I get to be my son's—or daughter's—dad."

"I'm not gonna run." Grant scowled. "Whether it's my kid or not. I'm not an asshole."

"Glad to hear it," Bailey said. She'd stepped back while the two men had jumped to their feet, but now she moved between them again. "Now, I don't want either of you giving Christina crap for this. We'll know which of you is the dad in a couple weeks, and that will be the end of it. She's going through a lot right now, so you two leave her alone, or you answer to *me*." Bailey poked her chest with her finger, her eyes, so like Christina's, filled with angry determination. She was a guard dog, warning them off her charge.

"It's all right, Bailey," Christina said. She stood up, her face too pale, shadows under her eyes, looking exhausted. Grant moved to her, liking that she gave him a grateful look when he put his arm around her.

"No, it's not," Bailey said. "Seriously, guys, don't mess with her."

Ray lifted his hands. "All right." He was angry. That showed in every line of his body, but Grant knew Ray. He'd never take out his anger on a woman. "What do I have to do?"

"When the time comes, go see Dr. Sue," Bailey said. "That's all. You too, Grant. Can you boys handle that?"

Grant gave her a nod, feeling hollow.

Ray clenched his fists. "Thanks for telling me, Christina," he said. "Think I'll be going now."

Without further word, Ray slammed out of the house, banging the door behind him. Grant waited to hear the sound of his truck but it didn't come.

A look out the window showed Ray striding away up the street, leaving his truck behind, as though he couldn't stop walking. Grant knew exactly how he felt.

Chapter Seventeen

"You okay?" Grant asked. He moved to Christina's side, warming her.

Christina wanted to fall into him and never come up. She wasn't okay at all. But then she was. This was a total mess, but ... *she was going to have a baby.*

Grant slid his arm around her, cradling her with his strength. "Bailey, could you give us a minute?"

Christina gave her sister a nod. "I'll be all right."

Bailey went to Grant and kissed his cheek. "Thanks, bro. For not being a dickhead."

Grant smiled a little. "Hey, no problem."

Bailey studied the two of them a moment then fetched her purse and walked out. Christina heard her get into her truck and drive away, most likely heading back to the Circle C Ranch, Adam, and her new life.

Thank God for Bailey. Christina's baby sister had helped her clear her head, figure out what she needed to do, and how to break the news to both men. Bailey had convinced her to talk to both at once, since Dr. Sue said the chances were equal that either had fathered her baby. Christina had decided they both needed to know at the same time.

But while she'd respect Ray's need to be a father to his child—both baby and Ray would deserve that—Christina knew she could never be with any man but Grant.

Grant and Christina sank to the sofa together, Grant's arm around her.

"I'm sorry," Christina said, her throat aching. "This is awful."

Grant pulled her closer. "I don't know. I've seen people go through worse shit than this. But no matter what happens, we'll face it together. All right?"

Christina looked up at him. Grant's eyes were warm, but she read the fear behind them.

Grant might say he'd be all right if the baby turned out to be Ray's, but would he, when it came down to it? Would he want to stay with Christina while she raised another man's kid? She couldn't imagine most men would.

"My life sucks," she said morosely.

"Everyone's does," Grant said. "Just in different ways."

That was possibly true.

"Now, I've got a lotta things to do," Grant said, his deep voice gentle. "I'm taking care of some stuff with Adam, but after that, we're going to talk. I mean for real. No losing control and having sex instead."

"Aw." Christina kept her face straight. "But losing control and having sex is more fun."

Grant's eyes twinkled. "Well, we can do that after. I know us, though. We get serious, and the next thing we know, we're throwing off our clothes and grabbing on to each other."

"All right." Christina gave him a grave nod. "Talk first. Sex second. We can try."

"That's my sugar bear." Grant scooped her close and kissed her cheek, his breath warm. "I swear to you, Christina. It's going to be all right."

She tried to smile. "Why? Because you say so?"

"You bet."

Grant trailed off but his arm stayed around her, his warm scent relaxing. Christina wanted to remain in this cocoon of peace with him until the weeks went by, and everything was settled. For better or for worse.

Grant pressed a kiss to the top of her head. She noticed he was avoiding kissing her on the mouth. That might lead to the loss of control he talked about.

"I have to go, sweetheart," he said. "You going to be all right here? I can tell Bailey to come back and stay with you if you want. Or Grace."

"Oh, for heaven's sake, I'll be fine." Christina softened the words by touching her lips to his cheek.

She shouldn't have. His warm skin and hot brush of whiskers made her want to run her tongue over him. She could undo his shirt, lick him some more, nibble his skin, suckle it …

Christina clenched her jaw and made herself pull away.

Grant's look told her he understood. "I can't guarantee I can stay out of your bed for long, sweetheart. But we'll get this figured out soon, hopefully before I burn up." He rose, pulled

Christina to her feet with him, and slid his arms around her. "I don't want to do anything but take care of you the rest of my life."

Christina rested her hands on his chest. "You keep talking like that, and I'll just let you."

Grant's look held heat, need, hope, and fear. "And I'll take you up on that."

He stepped away from her, picked up his hat, and left the house.

***

Grant tried to go on with life as usual, but everything had changed.

Sam Farrell, Christina's uncle, invited Grant around to talk. Grant thought he'd be chastised for letting Christina get pregnant—because everyone knew now—but what Sam said surprised him. The old guy had a lot of heart.

Ray helped Grant avoid awkward meetings with him by heading out of town with Kyle a few days later, back to the rodeo circuit. Word was that the two brothers kept on winning as usual—money, trophies, and sponsorships.

Even so, it was a tough two weeks. Grant woke up every morning wondering if he'd be the lucky man who'd hold his baby in his arms, or if he'd have to eat shit while watching Ray do it. He went to bed every night praying the kid was his. He'd dream it was, his heart swelling with happiness. Then the dream would change, and Ray and Christina, with child, would be sitting at the park in the town square, or wherever, a happy couple, while Grant could only stand by and watch.

Hell, no. Grant would have Christina with him forever. No matter what.

Meanwhile he and Christina had a standing date every night they could get free, at Mrs. Ward's for dinner. They talked — really talked, using the diner as neutral ground. No sex, no fighting, just getting to know each other again. It was refreshing.

The whole town knew Christina was pregnant, and most were speculating on whether the baby was Ray's or Grant's. Christina hadn't made any kind of announcement, but folks could count on their fingers and wonder. The fact that Grant and Christina seemed to be a couple again didn't calm the talk. But they could suck it up, Grant decided. He was sticking by Christina, whatever anyone thought.

Grant had other things going on during the nail-biting two weeks, though they had become more of a distraction now than anything else. Thankfully Adam and Carter had hammered everything out, with Grant and Tyler letting them.

This new business deal came to a head a few days before Christina was due to be tested, when Karen's ex-husband, Preston Waters, rolled into town. He was slim, well-groomed, and handsome in the obnoxious way of successful men who steam-rolled over everyone to get what they wanted.

Preston drove a tinted-windowed Lexus, which he was very careful of, and brought two assistants, a younger man every bit as obnoxious as himself, and a woman who dressed like Karen. The woman was younger than Karen and more arrogant.

Naively so, Grant thought when he met her. Life hadn't kicked her in the teeth yet.

Preston and his team met Karen, Grant, Adam, Carter, and Tyler in an upstairs room at the local bank for a little conference Carter had arranged. Mr. Carew, the head of the bank, was there too.

The room had a long table, cushioned chairs, and windows that looked out over the entire town of Riverbend and the rolling hills beyond. A beautiful, green backdrop under a brilliant blue sky.

Preston and his lackeys didn't hide their smirks as Grant and his brothers walked in. The Campbells and Carter wore black button-down shirts, jeans, and clean, polished cowboy boots, hats in hand. The four of them did own suits—they wore them to church and other formal occasions—but Grant had suggested that for this meeting they should look as cowboy as possible.

Karen joined them in one of her crisp linen business suits, her hair, makeup, and nails perfect as always.

"Preston," she said with cool neutrality, as she greeted the ex-husband who'd kept two mistresses under her nose.

"Karen," Preston said. "You remember Donald, and Candice."

"Candy, yes," Karen said absently. She'd told Grant that Candy had been one of the mistresses.

"Candice," the young woman clarified with steel in her voice. Candy had known about Karen and had been triumphant when Karen filed for divorce, so Christina had related to Grant. Though Preston hadn't married Candy, as apparently he'd promised, she was still holding out hope.

Karen ignored her. "Shall we get started? Let me introduce Adam, Grant, and Tyler Campbell, and Carter Sullivan."

"New entourage?" Preston asked, eyes sparkling with mirth. "You've gone native."

"Business partners," Karen said, smoothing her skirt as she took a seat. She utterly dismissed Preston and his thinly veiled hostility, as though the man himself didn't interest her in the least. Grant felt a bit of pride in Karen as she gave everyone at the table a look of cool indifference.

The young man called Donald sniggered. "Is that what they're calling it these days?"

Karen gave him a brief look that told him he was an idiot not much worth notice. Mr. Carew, the white-haired banker who'd run Riverbend's bank for decades, cleared his throat. "Can we get started?"

"Yes," Karen said in her brisk tone. "The purpose of this meeting is simple. You, Preston, are out of luck. The properties in and around Riverbend that you wished to develop are no longer for sale."

"Excuse me?" Preston's look was quizzical but unworried. "What are you talking about? I know *you* didn't buy them, Karen."

"The properties are in the process of being purchased from their owners by AGCT Enterprises," Karen said. "Any loans your mortgage brokerage bought are being paid off."

Preston stared at Karen in disbelief, then he started to go a little green. "I need to verify this."

Carter slid the stack of folders he'd brought with him across the table. "It's all right there."

Preston opened the top file, and his two assistants leaned in to examine the documents. "You can't do this," Preston said, looking up. "You don't have enough money to buy half the county."

"Not personally, no," Karen said. "But my new partners and I do collectively. Adam Campbell is worth millions, as is the Circle C Ranch, thanks to Carter and his brothers. Enough to purchase property in a small town in a depressed market. Just like you tried to do."

"You can't cut a deal out from under me, Karen," Preston snapped.

"I just did," Karen said smoothly. "AGCT Enterprises now owns most of the land that was going into foreclosure or about to be seized for tax liens. AGCT will lease or sell it back to the owners once the titles are cleared. If they want to build houses or open wine bars or B&Bs, that's their business. But I won't let you run all these people out of their cute town. I like it here."

Preston's gaze flickered over Adam, Grant, Carter, and Tyler who looked back at him, stone-faced.

"I think you like it a little *too* much," Preston said to Karen. "These guys look like something out of a B movie."

Karen folded her manicured hands. "Unlike *some* of the men I've known in my life, these cowboys are perfect gentlemen."

Preston made a very ungentlemanly snort. "All right, Karen. If this is what you want—you've won. This was a small-potatoes deal for me. Next time, watch out."

"There won't be any next time," Karen said. "I'm selling my part of the business. I'm finished with you, Preston. You're a cheap, lying, boring son of a bitch who thinks he can buy loyalty and friends. Well, you can't. You can walk into a diner and buy a piece of pie, but you can't buy the respect of everyone in the place."

Preston had no idea what she meant, that was clear. He got to his feet and shoved the folders back at Carter. His assistants scrambled up beside him.

"I'm out of here," Preston said. "This place stinks like horse shit anyway."

He shot a meaningful glance at the brothers, then stopped when Carter got up right in front of him.

Grant, Adam, and Tyler rose to flank Carter, but it was Carter who had Preston turning pale. Grant folded his arms and watched while Carter looked Preston up and down. No one could have meaner eyes than Carter Sullivan.

"What do you think, boys?" Carter asked his brothers, his voice deadly quiet. "Should we run him out of town?"

Grant drew his thumb and forefinger down the sides of his mouth. "I have a better idea. You got a rope?"

Preston swallowed, but gave a nervous laugh, as though trying to make himself believe they were joking with him. Grant and his brothers stood their ground.

Preston finally broke. He ducked around Carter and ran for the door, nearly running down Mr. Carew along the way. His assistants were already gone — they hadn't waited for him.

Adam closed the door behind Preston. Karen burst out laughing, one of the few sounds of true amusement Grant had ever heard her make.

"That was wonderful!" she crowed. She grabbed Grant and kissed his cheek, then Adam's, then Carter's and Tyler's without shame or fear. "Carter, you get the Oscar today. I've never seen Preston scared shitless before."

Tyler and Adam high-fived with both hands, and Grant clapped Carter on the back. "I love watching you do that," Grant said.

Carter remained straight-faced, but Grant could tell he was enjoying himself. "In that case, how about a beer?" Carter asked him. "You're buying."

"No, I am," Karen said, her smile wide. "You boys are awesome."

"And hey," Grant said. "We saved the town. Yeah, we are pretty awesome."

Carew shut files and gathered them up. "No, you're the same boys who think you can get away with everything by being smart-asses. Now get on out of here; I have work to do. Say hello to your mama for me."

Grant couldn't argue with him. He and his brothers walked out, Karen happy and smug, heading to the bar for an afternoon celebration. Grant, who'd started making sure he had his cell phone with him at all times, called Christina with the good news.

***

When the day came for the DNA testing, Grant went by himself to the clinic, getting in early to avoid an encounter with Ray. Dr. Sue said that everything had to be sent away to a lab, but she knew people there, and she'd have the results in a couple of days.

It was May now, and the temperatures had turned hot. A few days after Grant had gone for the test, his tension matched the weather. Black clouds piled up in the north and west, the heat promising storms to come.

Grant watched the clouds as he rode at the ranch, working a new horse at easy tasks. Hill Country didn't have many tornadoes, not like they did in west Texas, or up around Amarillo and Wichita Falls, but the weather could still be severe.

Grant had spent a summer in north Texas once. Every day they'd had a tornado watch, didn't matter that the afternoon started out clear and beautiful. By six, the sky could be black with clouds, everyone ready to head for shelter.

But while tornadoes were rare in Riverbed, hellacious thunderstorms and hailstorms were common. As the clouds rose and darkened the afternoon, the horse under him got cagey. Good sign bad weather was coming.

Grant quit training a little early so he'd have time to unsaddle and put the horse, haltered, into a wash rack. A quick rinse and a scrape was all the gelding needed, the air so hot the animal dried pretty fast. Grant finished rubbing him down, and then took him back to his stall. The stable hands were finished mucking for the day, and started replenishing the hay racks.

Grant ducked into the stables office as clouds blotted out the westering sun.

Carter, as usual, was going over the books, clicking around on his computer. "You meeting Christina for dinner tonight?" he asked.

"Yep," Grant said.

"Better go then," Carter said, without looking up. "Before this storm hits."

Carter liked to discuss the business or get Grant's input on upcoming projects after they finished for the day, but tonight he closed his mouth and said nothing. Carter knew what was important.

"That's what I had in mind," Grant said. "See ya."

He shucked his sweaty clothes for clean ones he kept at the ranch house, started up his truck and drove as quickly as he could into town. The wind kicked up and the first drops of rain spattered on his window as he parked and hurried into the diner.

Shutting out the wind and inhaling the aroma of good food made him feel fine. Even better was Christina waiting in their booth, a warm smile on her face.

They'd been going out like this—taking it in easy paces—for the last two weeks. Having dinner together. Walking under the stars. Christina coming out to watch him ride, sitting in the shade of the covered arena, while Grant trained. Talking about how Christina was feeling with the baby, evading questions from everyone else in town about it.

Sometimes he and Christina drove up the highway to the one movie theater in River County to watch the latest releases. Not just chick movies— Christina enjoyed edge-of-seat action-adventure thrillers as much as Grant did.

Or they'd sit on the porch either at the ranch or Christina's house. At the ranch they were surrounded by family, banter, and laughter.

At Christina's they'd sit quietly on the porch, holding hands, before they went into the house to spend the night together. If Christina didn't feel well, they'd simply lie entwined in the dark. The nights Christina was energetic, they made love as though they'd never stop.

It was a sparkling time, a special time. Grant and Christina came together without heat. No going over the hurts of the past, no speculating about the future.

The future was coming up on them fast, though. Tomorrow, Dr. Sue had said, it would all be clear.

Grant had a box in his pocket he wanted to bring out, but he was waiting until they knew, so Christina could decide, without doubt, what she wanted to do.

"You just made it," Christina said, watching the rain spatter the windows. "I ordered you an iced tea. Unsweetened, no lemon."

Just as he liked it. "Great. Thanks."

This was what marriage would be. Meeting up after work, planning the evening, Christina knowing exactly what Grant wanted to eat and drink. Talking about little things no one else would care about, no drama or trying to perform for each other.

Just love and intense happiness.

The rain fell harder. Grant glanced out the window and was no longer able to see across the parking lot. Then came a pounding on the roof as the rain turned white.

"Hail, yeah!" someone in the restaurant yelled.

Christina rolled her eyes. "That was only funny the first twenty times I heard him say it."

"Clint needs new material," Grant agreed. "Hey, tomorrow, you know … after …" After they learned the test results. "Why don't we take a drive? Maybe go out to LBJ, have a picnic, take a boat out. You know, kid stuff."

He didn't have to add *if the weather's better,* because this storm would be long gone by morning. At the moment, though, the hail pounded down outside, two-inch chunks of ice that bounced off cars and the asphalt, slamming into the windows, which fortunately held.

"Sure." Christina gave him a strong smile, the one that made her beautiful. "Maybe you'll go swimming, and I can see you in a thong."

Grant barked a laugh. "Yeah, right. In what universe?"

"You have a nice ass. I'd pay to see you walking around the shore in nothing but a teeny little piece of fabric."

Grant leaned toward her. "You don't have to pay, baby. I'll do you a striptease for free."

"Not in my restaurant," Mrs. Ward said, halting by their table. "Once you're out of here, what you do is your business. Now, what can I get you two?"

At that moment, someone in the back yelled, and curses rolled from the kitchen.

Mrs. Ward's brows slammed together. "I've been having some leaks. The roofers swear they fixed them all, but this is what happens when you have flat roofs and Texas rains."

"Why don't you go take care of that?" Grant asked, his face still warm from being caught offering the striptease.

"You two want your usual?" Mrs. Ward asked, poised to go.

"That would be great," Christina said.

Mrs. Ward hustled away, her voice rising as she reached the kitchen. "What the *hell*? You call those people and tell them ..."

"We might have rainwater on our steaks," Grant said. "Doesn't matter." He reached over and took Christina's hand. She squeezed his fingers. "As long as we're here together, having fun."

Christina opened her mouth to answer. Whatever she'd been about to say, Grant never knew, because at that moment, the entire roof groaned. Plaster crashed down from above followed by a torrent of dirt and water.

Grant was out of the booth the second he saw plaster dust in his iced tea. He grabbed Christina and yanked her down with him, shoving her under the table moments before the entire section of the ceiling collapsed.

Chapter Eighteen

Christina yelped as Grant landed on top of her, pressing her into the cold vinyl floor. Ceiling tiles, bolts, and pieces of metal poured around them, followed by the water that had built up on the roof to send it smashing down.

The place had gone dark, fuses blowing. People screamed. One man yelled into a cell phone, calling for the fire department.

Christina held on to Grant as his back took the bulk of the mess.

"You okay?" he kept saying. "You okay, Christina?"

He wiped dirt from her face. The deluge finally eased but didn't completely cease, a constant patter taking its place.

"I'm going to climb out," Grant said in her ear. "Hang on to me; I'll get you through."

Christina complied. Grant backed out from under the booth, throwing off pieces of ceiling tile as he went. He kicked and cleared debris away, as others were doing, then set Christina on her feet.

The downpour of ceiling tile and water had stopped, but the roof was still making noises Christina didn't like.

Mrs. Ward's voice sounded over the din. "If you can all go out the back door and get to the store, we can take shelter there. Keep the street and parking lot clear for the emergency crews. Anyone hurt?"

No one admitted to being, though one child cried loudly.

"Come on." Grant had his arm around Christina's waist.

He guided her out the back door, both of them wincing as the hail came down. The downpour had lightened the slightest bit, but the hailstones stung where they stuck.

Grant's truck was close, but if the hail grew heavy again, they wouldn't necessarily be safe inside the cab. Hail could break windows and destroy vehicles in a heartbeat.

The convenience store, a much newer structure, had tall, solid awnings, and a thick-walled, windowless storage room that doubled as a tornado shelter. They could wait it out there.

Halfway across the slippery, cold, crowded parking lot, Christina felt a sharp pain in her abdomen. She gasped, but it went away as rapidly as it had come. She said nothing until it happened again—a cramp that twisted her insides and made her want to double over.

Fear as icy as the hail washed over her. "Grant!" she said in a panic.

Grant caught the terror in her voice. "What is it, sweetie? What's wrong?"

"I need to go to the hospital." Christina's words caught, her throat tight. "Right now."

Grant didn't need to ask a barrage of questions. He understood.

He looked up and down the street, but there was no sign of any fire truck or ambulance yet. Emergency vehicles had to come in from the highway, and the roads were white with falling hail.

"Shit," Grant said, then started for his truck. "Come on."

A couple of people tried to stop them and ask what the matter was, but Grant simply shouldered his way through. He got Christina into the truck and cranked it to life.

The patrons from the diner were hurrying through the north side of the parking lot, making for the store, so Grant squealed off to the south driveway, which led them in the opposite direction they needed to go. He drove as fast as he could around three sides of the courthouse square to the north road, and headed out of town.

"Hang on, sweetheart," Grant said, and drove directly into the storm.

Christina nodded. After the last pain, the cramps had subsided, but she clenched the seat, terrified they would return.

She couldn't lose this baby. She couldn't. Christina knew in her heart that if she didn't bring this baby to term, she'd never have the chance to have another.

Maybe it just wasn't meant to be.

"No," Christina sobbed.

Grant set his warm hand over her closed one. "I'm going to get you there all right, sugar. I'm not going to let anything happen to you, you got it?"

Christina nodded tightly again.

The truck spun as Grant took the corner to the highway, but he steadied it with an easy touch. No one else was on the road; the pavement was empty and gleaming in the dark.

Lightning filled the sky, and thunder boomed on top of it. The hail thickened, beating on the roof until the din blotted out all other sound.

Christina sucked in a breath as the truck slid again. "Grant, you are *crazy!*"

Grant let go of her hand to crank the steering wheel until they came out of the skid. "I am, but I'm good at what I do. I'm not losing you!"

"You won't!" Christina yelled over the hail. "Not ever." They were meant to be together—all this stuff shoving them toward each other couldn't be a coincidence.

Call it God or destiny or the grand scheme of the universe, any event that had tried to tear them apart hadn't been able to part them forever. They came back, like two ends of a stretched rubber band. Didn't matter how far forces pulled them, they'd snap back together in the end. And who was Christina to defy the universe?

"Hot damn!" Grant shouted in response.

Hail blotted out almost everything, including the yellow line in the middle of the road, the brush on either side of it. Grant's headlights glittered on falling ice.

Christina shouted, "You know, if we wreck on the way, none of this will matter."

"We won't. Hang on!"

The truck spun again, and again, Grant calmly righted it. He knew this vehicle well, and coaxed it to work like he wooed his horses.

Christina laughed out loud. In spite of her absolute fear and this wild weather, Grant was taking care of her, just like he always did.

"I love you, Grant Campbell!" she said at the top of her voice. "Will you marry me?"

"What?" Grant stared at her a split second before he swung back to peer down the road.

"I said, will you marry me?"

"Shit, woman!"

"Is that a no?" Christina was shaking all over from terror and adrenaline rush. "Because I'm not taking no for an answer."

"Damn it all to hell, baby, I'm supposed to be asking *you* that."

"Then why haven't you?" Christina reached out and put her hand on his warm thigh — not enough to distract him, but because she needed to be touching him. "It's not like I'm going anywhere!"

"Because I thought you'd want to wait. You know — to find out."

She laughed again, her laughter tinged with hysteria. "I thought *you* wanted to wait. So you could decide whether to leave."

"I'm not going anywhere, either!" Grant yelled at her. "But I swear to you I'm ready to pop the question. I have a box in my pocket with your Aunt Caroline's engagement ring. Your uncle gave it to me."

Christina stared. "What?"

"I said, your uncle ..."

"I heard you. I mean, *why*?"

"'Cause he loves you, I guess. He gave me the ring and said I should ask you, because we belong together. We always have. He said that being apart for the last year was just us getting our heads out of our asses."

"Wait, my uncle really said *getting our heads out of our asses*?"

"Not in so many words." Grant's mouth twitched, but his body was stiff with tension. "But I know what he meant. No matter how much we're apart, we're still together. Why not make it official?"

"Karen said the same thing."

Grant barked a laugh. "Good old Karen. Mrs. Kaye did too."

"Well, then—if everyone in town thinks we should get married, why don't we?"

"All right then." Grant got the truck around a bend in the road without sliding. "Yes, damn it, I'll marry you!"

Christina clapped her arm over her abdomen as another cramp came, not as bad this time, but even so, scary as hell. "I love you, Grant," she gasped.

"I love you too, baby. Hang on."

The slackening hail became heavy rain as Grant swung into the parking lot of the clinic. He screeched to a halt at the emergency room doors and ran around to help her inside.

An orderly saw them stumble toward the door, came out with a wheelchair, a nurse with a clipboard following.

"We got her," the nurse said. She knew Grant and his family by name. "You go park, Mr. Campbell. We'll take care of her."

Christina gave him a nod. Grant stood like a man pole-axed, his face gray, as he watched Christina be wheeled inside the clinic, and then out of sight.

***

Grant waited for news. He sat in the stiff chairs of the waiting room he'd reposed in so often over the years when his brothers were brought in for injuries, or else he paced in the open area before the elevator.

Time crawled. Whenever he looked at his watch, he found that only one or two minutes had gone by since the last time he'd checked. This was turning into one of the longest nights of his life.

Grant had called his mom and told her what happened. No, she shouldn't come out there, he said, and neither should Bailey. The roads were way too dangerous. He'd keep them posted, and when the weather let up, they could drive over.

Outside the long windows, the sky lit top to bottom with streaks of lightning as the storm marched across the plains to the river. Rain filmed the windows, and the occasional handful of hail spattered out of the darkness into the glass.

Grant waited. The box with the ring was heavy in his jacket pocket, the jacket itself soaked with water. But the ring was safe. He'd made sure of that.

Two hours went by at a snail's pace. The rain calmed, but wind bent the small trees in the parking lot and lightning flickered against blackness.

"Mr. Campbell," a nurse said. "Come on back. She's asking for you."

Grant nearly ran for the corridor past the nurse's station — the nurse had to hurry to get ahead of him.

"She all right?" Grant didn't wait for an answer but charged into Christina's room.

Christina lay back against the half-raised bed. Her face was bloodless, but her eyes didn't show the haunted look he'd feared.

"You okay?" Grant asked, afraid of the answer.

Christina gave him a faint smile and slid her hand to her abdomen. "We're both all right."

"Thank God," Grant said fervently. He'd never said a truer prayer in his life. He dropped to the chair next to her bed, his head going to his hands. "Thank God."

"They checked me over really well," Christina said. "Dr. Sue is here, so she did it herself. She said I was way stressed, and they need to watch me tonight, but the baby is okay. But with the ceiling falling on me, surviving a hair-raising ride through one of the worst storms in years ... I need to take it easy. But I'm all right. I'm pretty tough."

"I told you I'd get you here safe." Grant let out his breath. "I was so damn scared, Christina."

"Yeah?" Christina's smile shook. "Well, I was flipping terrified." She lifted her hand, palm out, to him. "Let me see it."

"See what?"

"The ring, sweet-ass. I want us engaged before I walk out of here."

Grant's grin came from a place of warmth. He lifted his wet denim jacket, removed a small box from the pocket, and opened it.

On a fold of tissue paper lay a simple and beautiful ring. A gold band held a round diamond flanked on four sides by diamond chips. The ring shone softly, burnished by time.

Grant drew the chair next to the high bed. He settled one knee on the chair seat and took the ring from the box.

"Christina Farrell," he said. "Will you do me the honor of becoming my wife?"

Christina's brown eyes shone with tears. "Are you sure you're sure? What about ..." She touched her abdomen. "What if the baby isn't yours? Will you really want marriage to me then?"

Grant closed his strong hand over Christina's. "What I want is *you*. I know the kid might be Ray's. I know if it is, it probably means I can't have kids at all. But we can adopt kids, have as big a family as we want. Hell, Carter's adopted, and he turned out all right. And if this baby *is* Ray's, the poor kid's gonna be stuck with two dads."

Christina burst out laughing, even while tears trickle down her face. "I was thinking the same things. I love you Grant Campbell. I will marry you. I will, I will, I will, I will."

Her smile took Grant's breath away. A wave of happiness broke over him, a sense that everything was in its right place in the world. Didn't matter what they had to face, they'd face it together.

Grant took Christina's warm left hand in his and slid the ring onto her third finger. The ring fit like it was made for her.

He leaned down and kissed his Christina. The sweetest kiss, the one Grant had been waiting for all his life.

"What the hell?"

Grant came up swiftly at the sound of Ray Malory's voice. Ray stood in the doorway, the nurse who'd brought Grant in trying to keep him out.

"Ray," Christina said in surprise. Then she made a reassuring motion to the nurse. "It's all right. He's just worried about me."

The nurse frowned. "Maybe, but your doctor said you needed rest, and too many visitors will over-stress you." She gave Ray a severe look. "Talk quick. Then you need to go."

"They said at the diner you were hurt," Ray said to Christina after the nurse had left them. "And that Grant had driven you out of there like the devil running out of hell. I was afraid ... afraid ..."

"The baby's fine," Christina said, giving him a smile. "Just fine. Grant got me here quick enough, through a wild hailstorm."

Ray glared at Grant as though he wanted to throw him to the floor. Grant made himself not respond. Ray must have been just as scared as he'd been for Christina and the baby. At this point, Ray had as much to lose as Grant.

Ray's hair and shirt was all wet—he'd come through the storm too. For Christina.

"It's probably a good thing you're here," Christina said, her voice losing its energy. "Dr. Sue said she got the test results back late this afternoon. She was going to call me in the morning, but she said she'd give them to me tonight if we wanted to know now."

Grant's tension ramped back up. To know. Tonight.

Now that it came down to it, Grant didn't want the truth. He wasn't sure he could handle it.

Maybe it was a family trait, not being able to make kids. Adam—before Bailey—and Tyler had never been able to keep it in their pants, and they didn't have a string of women holding up babies whenever they walked by. The only one of them who had a kid was Carter, and he wasn't a Campbell by blood.

No, Grant needed to know this. To take it in the gut. The knowledge would change Grant's life, but he needed to face it.

He saw that Ray was going through the same dilemma. Ray's face was drawn and pasty, as though he suffered from a three-day hangover.

"Yeah," Ray said. "Let's get this over with."

Grant nodded tightly.

Christina rang for the nurse and asked her if Dr. Sue would come down. The nurse looked alarmed at first, but Christina told her that Dr. Sue was waiting for her call.

If Grant had thought the two hours waiting to see if Christina was okay had been the longest of his life, the twenty minutes waiting for Dr. Sue competed for the title.

Ray paced, arms folded. Grant stayed by Christina's side, holding her hand until she kissed his closed fist and told him he was making her fingers stiff.

Dr. Sue came in, saw both men, and said, "Ah."

"Just tell us," Ray growled. "We're going crazy."

"Well, I don't know myself," Dr. Sue said. She handed Christina the envelope she carried. "It's Christina's business. She sees it first."

A swallow moved down Christina's throat as she reached a shaking hand for the envelope. She settled it on the blankets, fighting with the pulse monitor on her finger before she tore the seal with her thumb and pulled out a sheaf of papers.

Christina read the first page, flipped to the second, and frowned.

"Well?" Grant realized he'd stopped breathing. "What the hell does it say?"

"It says ..." Christina cleared her throat. "Subject one—Grant—cannot be ruled out as the biological father."

Grant blinked, turning the weird sentence around in his head. "What the hell does that mean?"

Ray glared at him. "It means you're the father, dumb-ass."

"Yes," Dr. Sue said briskly. "That's exactly what it means."

Grant remained in place for a few seconds as his brain caught up and the revelation seeped through his body.

He let out a whoop that drowned out the next clap of thunder.

"Whoo-hoo! I'm having a *baby*! I'm going to be a dad!" Grant left the floor, punching the air with both fists. "I'm a *dad*!"

Christina was laughing and crying, wiping her eyes with the envelope. Dr. Sue watched them all, quiet with experience, a smile on her face.

Ray didn't say a word. He'd turned his back, arms jammed across his chest. Grant looked over Christina's shoulder at the other paper lying on her lap. *Subject Two — Ray — ruled out as the biological father.*

No doubt about it.

"Ray," Grant said.

Ray lifted his head and turned around. His eyes were wet. "Congratulations, Grant. Christina. This was for the best, I guess. You two need to be together. Now you can be—totally."

"Ray, I'm sorry," Christina said softly. "I'm sorry I put you through this."

Ray shook his head. He didn't look at either of them, but moisture glittered on his lashes. "I'd have wanted to know. I'll see you."

Without waiting for argument or good-byes, Ray swung around and left the room.

Dr. Sue put her hands into the pockets of her white coat. "That's that, then. Congratulations, you two." She glanced at the ring sparkling on Christina's finger. "Double congrats. When's the wedding?"

Grant and Christina both started to talk, then Christina laughed. Grant answered. "As soon as humanly possible. All right, Christina?"

"Fine by me," Christina said. She lay back, looking suddenly exhausted. "But I get a pretty dress. And a church. Oh, man, Bailey's going to kill me when I tell her she only has a few weeks to plan the wedding."

Dr. Sue gestured with her hands in her pockets, the coat opening and closing. "Sounds like you have it covered. Now, I'll let you kiss her good-night, Grant, and you can sleep here at the clinic if you want, but she has to rest."

"You got it, Doc."

Grant didn't wait until Dr. Sue left to begin the kissing. He needed Christina's kisses right now.

Christina laughed as he leaned over her, and Grant tasted the laughter in his mouth.

Christina was his. He had a family. Grant placed his hand over Christina's abdomen. She slid her hand on top of his, her touch light but strong.

Her kisses were the same. She was fragile, his Christina, but she'd make it. She'd already proved she could put up with Grant and all his shit through good times and bad.

Grant deepened the kiss, Christina's hand coming up to cup his neck.

There would be all good times from now on. Sexy times, fun times, happy times — and full of love.

Because now they were three.

Chapter Nineteen

Three weeks later

...   Three   weeks   of   planning,   whirlwind
preparation, doctor's appointments, and crazy days.

Bailey, Christina and their mother, who was
thrilled to be marrying off another daughter so soon,
worked long hours to make this wedding as elegant
as Bailey's had been in a fraction of the time.

Again the reception would be at Circle C Ranch,
and Grace volunteered to cook most of the food. She
loved her new job as chef for the ranch and partial
nanny to Faith.

Mrs. Ward offered to send out a host of pies for
the   occasion   full   of   late   spring   goodness —
strawberry, rhubarb, early summer berries.

Her restaurant had been closed of course, because
of all the damage, but thankfully, no one had been
hurt. Mrs. Ward had insurance on the place, but the
collapse broke her heart. Christina thought Karen

might step in and try to buy the place again, but she did not.

Instead, Carter visited Mrs. Ward and told her that AGCT Enterprises would invest in helping her get back on her feet. That's what the new company did—invested in Riverbend and kept its heritage alive. Grant and Adam were the founders of the organization, Carter kept the books, Tyler was PR, and Karen was on the board to look around for things to invest in.

Karen was becoming very fond of Riverbend, and was even looking for a place to live. She'd be adopting a central Texas accent before long, Christina thought, and pretend she'd lived there all her life.

Ray Malory dealt with the discovery that he was not the father of Christina's child by leaving town, with the excuse that there were more rodeos out there, more prizes to be won. It was his job.

Christina felt bad for everything she'd put him through, though Kyle told her she shouldn't.

"He's a big boy," Kyle said to Christina one night at the bar. "He's disappointed, and I can't blame him, but he'll be all right. Trust me. He's drowning his sorrows in the sweeties who are all over him at the rodeos. Give him time."

"I shouldn't have gone out with him at all," Christina said. She'd started as manager, finding she liked making all the decisions for the place. She'd been taking a break with a glass of apple juice when Kyle had come to say hello. "I should have known I'd never get over Grant."

"Well, Ray knew that—we all did—but he went out with you anyway. It's not entirely your fault,

Christina." Kyle put a kind hand on her shoulder. "Plus, he could have used a condom."

Christina had laughed and kissed Kyle on the cheek.

She'd always feel remorse that her old friend Ray had gotten hurt in her mess with Grant, but Christina allowed herself to enter the euphoria that had come into her life. She was marrying the hottest cowboy in Texas, the one she loved to pieces, and they were having a baby together.

On a fine Saturday in the first part of June, Christina met Grant at the church in Riverbend. She wore a lacy white dress that floated around her, Bailey as her matron of honor in soft blue, Faith in a matching blue dress as a flower girl.

Grant and his brothers were in tuxes again, with cowboy boots. This time Grant waited at the altar, Adam beside him, Grant's blue eyes warming when he saw Christina walking sedately up the aisle on her father's arm.

Christina paused on the way to press a kiss to Sam Farrell's lined face, then continued until she was handed to Grant.

It was a beautiful Texas Hill Country day. Warm but not too hot, white clouds floating across the sunny sky. Grant and Christina held each other's hands and looked straight into each other's eyes when they said *I do.*

Christina wore no veil, only a sprig of flowers in her hair, so all Grant had to do was tilt her face to his and kiss her.

And kiss her. Grant's mouth opened hers, his hands pressing her into him. Christina tasted his joy, felt his strength as he bent over her, cradling her in warmth that wouldn't stop.

Neither did the kiss. Tyler whooped, then every cowboy in the place followed suit.

When Grant finally released Christina and stood her upright, she was out of breath. Grant raised his fist to his brothers and friends in victory, and Christina gave them a thumb's up.

Walking back down the aisle with him, arm in arm, was minus the pain it had been at Bailey's wedding. A lot had happened since then that had lifted Christina up, shaken her, and set her back down again.

She clung to Grant's strong arm as he nearly ran with her to the end of the aisle. Grant looked down at her, sending Christina his hot, wicked smile.

She'd found her happily ever after.

***

The reception was the wildest party Riverbend had known in a while. Grant made sure of it.

He even made sure Kyle and Ray were there—no hard feelings. Ray hadn't brought a date, but the look of raw pain Grant had seen in him at the hospital had eased. Now he looked more at peace, ready to move on.

Kyle, on the other hand, had been pissed off at Grant all spring, ever since Grace had announced she was working at the Circle C.

"You think you're funny, don't you?" Kyle asked as he stood with Grant at the edge of the dance floor. "Getting Grace a job *working for your ranch*?"

"She loves it," Grant said. "She's settling in real nice."

"I know she loves it," Kyle growled. "I haven't seen her so happy in a long time."

"Then, you're welcome."

Kyle scowled at him. "You know damn well why I don't want her at your house."

"Because of Carter," Grant said. "I figured out pretty quick that's why you tried to fix me up with her. But there's nothing wrong with Carter, my friend. He's smart, generous, and trustworthy as hell. My mom saw all that in him when he was a kid, and made sure it was able to come out. Plus, he's proved he makes a great dad."

"I know." Kyle looked embarrassed. "It's just … his past might come back to bite him, and I wouldn't want my sister caught in it. Let me put it another way—if Christina had started going out with Carter, what would you have done?"

"Killed him," Grant said, his cheerfulness returning. He snagged a beer from a passing tray. "Give him a break, Kyle. Carter's a good guy. He can take care of his past. Besides, Faith loves Grace. Let's not mess with that."

Kyle let out a breath. "Right. I'll try."

"Carter can barely say two words to her." Grant gestured with the bottle to Carter, who was standing by himself. Carter's gaze was on Grace in her light summer dress as she talked animatedly with Bailey, Christina, and Lucy.

"I see that," Kyle said, sounding more hopeful. "Maybe it will come to nothing."

"Or maybe they'll find out they were meant for each other. Like me and Christina."

Kyle unbent enough to laugh. "Shit, if we have to go through watching another relationship like yours and Christina's, I think we'll all move away."

"Screw you," Grant said good-naturedly. "Excuse me, I need to go put my arms around my wife."

"Yeah." Kyle tipped his beer in a toast. "Already tied to the apron strings."

"What a great idea." Grant's imagination went to a sinful place. "I'll ask Christina if she has an apron …"

"Just go away."

Grant clicked his beer against Kyle's and strolled off on light feet.

The girls were having a feminine conversation involving much laughter, sly glances at the Campbell men, and apparently an argument with Bailey.

"Yes, you should," Christina was saying. "I'll drag you up there, Bailey. I'm your big sister—you have to do what I tell you."

"Since when?" Bailey asked in mock indignation. "It's your day Christina. I'll have mine later."

"Bull," Christina said. "We're telling everyone."

"Telling everyone what?" Grant asked, sliding his arm around Christina.

The four women burst into giggles, Bailey red-faced. Christina rose on tiptoe and whispered into Grant's ear.

Christina's warm breath tickling inside him went straight to Grant's cock, but he made himself pay attention to her words. When she finished, Grant raised his head.

"Really?" he said to Bailey. He grabbed her hand. "Forget hiding your light under a bushel—come on."

"Grant—"

Bailey broke off as Christina took her other hand. "Adam!" Grant called to Adam, who was in a knot with Tyler and Ross. "Get over here. We have an announcement to make."

Adam, mystified, came to them quickly, rescuing Bailey from Grant. Grant waved the musicians to a halt and took the microphone.

"Hey, ya'll," he said.

Everyone turned around. The whole town was there, including Karen, who'd brought another cowboy with her. He was about five years younger than her, and very fit. The woman was shameless.

There was applause, raised glasses, and expectant looks.

Grant said, "I want to thank y'all for coming out and saying hey to me and Christina, now that we finally got our butts up the aisle."

Laughter, cheers, whoops. "About time!" Tyler yelled.

"Now, my brother Adam, because he always has to upstage me, has an announcement to make."

Grant shoved the microphone at a startled Adam. Adam glared at him, and Bailey whispered, "Grant, *no.*"

"Come on, Adam," Grant said, leaning so his words went into the mike. "Say it like man."

Adam intensified the glare, grabbed the mike, and made a show of pushing Grant out of the way. Then he took Bailey's hand and kissed it.

"Me and Bailey are having a baby," Adam announced.

Silence. Then the big tent erupted into cheers, applause, a lot of *aws*.

Carter raised his beer to them, the quiet smile on his face as warm as Tyler's crazed yells. Faith jumped up and down and clapped. "I get cousins. I get cousins!"

Grant seized the mike back from Adam. "So are me and Christina," he said. "But y'all already knew that."

More laughter, clapping. Grant waved at the band to start playing again. "Adam," he said before he relinquished the mike to the band leader. "Dance with your wife."

Grant caught Christina, who was two steps from him, and pulled her into his arms. As couples, including Adam and Bailey, began spinning around them, he whispered, "I love you."

"I love *you*." Christina slid her hands to his shoulders, her smile igniting everything good inside him. "And I love how great you are to your brothers."

Grant grinned. "Not that they always deserve it."

"Doesn't matter. You're all about family, and not too macho to admit it."

"You love family too, baby. *And* you're a firecracker in bed. How'd I get so lucky?"

Christina shrugged as she wrapped her arms around him. "You have an angel on your shoulder, I guess."

"No, I got one rubbing against my front." Grant loved that Christina wasn't demure and shy. She said what she meant, but she was always about truth.

Plus she had no qualms about giving him hot looks that promised a lot of sparks later.

"Maybe we can find a tree to get stuck to," she said slyly as they began moving in the dance.

Grant kissed her cheek. "How about our big, soft bed at your house? We'll get in it tonight, and we won't get out until we're good and ready. Even if it's three days later."

"Sounds great." Christina drew herself closer, rose on tiptoe, and nibbled his earlobe. "But we can see what we can do under that tree first, can't we?"

Grant's entire body went tight. "Sugar, you are one wicked woman."

"Aw, you wouldn't like me if I weren't." Christina bit his ear again, then drew away.

"Hell, baby, I'd love you no matter what you were like, and you know it."

Grant took her hands and led her out through the whirling couples. Many people wanted to stop and talk, congratulate, hug, and Grant and Christina let them.

Then, when Grant saw an opening, he grabbed Christina's hand and ran with her out into the cool, moonlit air.

Down the hill they went, their laughter floating into the night. Behind them their families and friends of Riverbend danced in the glow of the tent, and Christina's flowers fell to the grass to glitter in the darkness like white stars.

End

Please continue for a preview of

Riding Hard: Carter

**Book 3
of the**

Riding Hard series

by

Jennifer Ashley

Carter

Chapter One

Grace Malory opened the oven door, filling the large kitchen at the Campbells' ranch with the warm aroma of baking cake.

She worked alone in the family kitchen today, so she heard no applause, no sounds of appreciation. Her nose, though, told her that the cake had come out just fine.

Grabbing pot holders, she lifted the cake from the oven and set it on waiting cooling racks on the counter. She turned off the stove, threw down the pot holders, and breathed a sigh of relief.

This cake needed to be perfect. It was for Faith's birthday tomorrow—Grace had volunteered to make all the goodies for her party, including a special cake that would hold nine candles.

Faith had requested a Texas sheet cake— "The kind with chocolate frosting," Faith had said, wrinkling her fine-boned nose. "Not the frosting with all the nuts in it. Please?"

"Of course, sweetie," Grace had said. "It's your birthday. You can have what you want."

Faith was in a *no nuts on anything or in anything* phase. No raisins either. Faith liked to eat both of those, but not mixed in with her cakes, cookies, pies, or what-have-you. "I like nuts in the shells, and raisins in the box," Faith had declared.

"As God intended," her father, Carter had rumbled in response. Faith had laughed in delight, and Grace had looked on, her heart flip-flopping.

Grace leaned down to inhale the cake's fragrance, once more satisfied. It unnerved her that it was Carter's praise she imagined when the finished, frosted masterpiece was laid before Faith and her friends tomorrow. Carter so rarely gave his approval to anyone but his daughter that winning some from him was all the sweeter.

Grace knew full well that she wanted Carter to look at her for more reasons than the triumph of pleasing a hard-to-please man. She wanted his intense hazel-eyed gaze on her, while he gave her his slow nod.

To hell with it. She just wanted to be in the same *room* with the man, no matter what he said or did. *Pathetic.*

Grace slammed open her notebook, flipping to the sheet cake frosting recipe she'd perfected for Faith. Her recipe notebook was thick with cakes, cookies, and pastries of all kinds, which she'd created and mastered when she'd planned to open a restaurant with another chef who turned out to be a crook. All Grace's hopes and dreams had flown when the man had disappeared in the night with all the funds, *after* Grace had made a down payment on the restaurant and co-signed for a start-up loan.

She'd been shocked, betrayed, financially devastated, and plain mad. Being all-around cook to a local ranching family wasn't her end goal, but when Grant, the second oldest Campbell brother had suggested it, Grace leapt at the chance.

Because I need the money, Grace had told herself. She was stuck paying back the loans the con man had left her with. *And something to do to take my mind off things.*

Bull. She'd jumped at the offer to work here so she'd have an excuse to be near Carter Sullivan, the Campbells' adopted brother. She'd been gone on him since high school, when he'd been the cool kid, untouchable and mysterious.

At first, Grace had thought her crush had stemmed from the fact that Carter was forbidden fruit, but over the years, she'd changed her mind. She simply liked *him,* everything about him—from his Houston drawl, to his long silences, to his hard face and the tatts that laced down his arms. And, all right, his hot body and great ass.

But the man never noticed her.

A thump on the kitchen door broke Grace out of her contemplation. She'd been staring at the recipe while she daydreamed about Carter and not seeing a word of it.

No one was home at the Campbell house—the family was out and about doing various things that took them to the far corners of River County, and Faith was at school. It was a fine September day, with a blue arch of sky and floating white clouds, warm but not too hot. Perfect weather.

The guys—and a few gals—who worked down in the stables rarely came to the house, calling on the phone when they needed something. But maybe they'd smelled baking and come looking for something to eat. They knew Grace liked feeding people.

Grace closed her notebook and moved across the kitchen floor to the little alcove that led to the back door.

"Grace's Kitchen," she sang as she flung the door open. "How can I help … ?"

Her words died as she took in the woman on the doorstep. Grace had no idea who she was, which was odd, because Grace knew everyone in Riverbend.

The woman was on the small side, about an inch shorter than Grace, and very slender. She wore stained jeans and a black, close fitting tank top with wide shoulder straps, and carried a leather jacket slung over one arm.

Her hair was short and spiky, dyed a flat, soot black. She wore no makeup on her pale face, the lines about her eyes incongruous with her apparent youth. She had lines around her mouth too, and a pinched look that Grace thought, but wasn't sure, came from certain types of addictive drugs.

"I'm sorry," Grace said, the politeness she'd learned at her mother's knee coming to her rescue. "I thought it was one of the stablemen coming to ask for a sandwich. Were you looking for someone?"

The woman already made her uncomfortable, but Grace refused to let herself judge too quickly. She might simply have gotten lost on the back highways that crisscrossed Hill Country and need directions.

The woman looked Grace up and down with hard, brown eyes. Grace did *not* know her, yet there was something familiar about those eyes, in the shape of them and the way they narrowed.

"Who are you?" the woman snapped. Her voice was gravelly, too deep for such a young throat.

"I'm the cook," Grace said. "I work here." Normally, Grace was far friendlier, offering her name and her life story to anyone she met, but her instincts were telling her to be reticent.

"Carter still live here?"

"Yes," Grace said slowly. Lying would do no good—the woman could ask anyone in town that question and get the same answer. "But he's not here. Can I tell him who stopped by?"

"You his wife?" The woman gave her a surly stare.

"No." Grace's wariness grew, straining her politeness. "As I said, I cook for the family. They're out today, but if you want to leave a message, I'll see that they get it."

"Where's the girl?"

Grace blinked. "Girl?"

"He named her Faith. Dumbass named her that to get back at me."

Grace blinked few more times, then she remembered where she'd seen eyes that shape, a mirror of the expression in them.

Holy shit, she was Lizzie Fredrickson. Faith's mother.

"Um," Grace said, finding her voice. "She's not here."

"Where the hell is she then?" The voice was harsh, filled with volumes of rage.

Nine years ago, this woman had come to the house, shoved a bundle into Carter's arms, and taken off down the road. The bundle had contained a newborn baby, screaming with fear at the enormity of the world.

Carter had been in complete shock, but once he realized the baby was indeed his, he'd devoted himself fiercely to taking care of her.

And now Lizzie had come back, asking for Faith.

Grace's own anger grew. She'd watched how Carter had struggled, still a kid himself at eighteen, to be a father, and a good one. He'd given up a lot to make sure Faith was taken care of, kept safe, loved. He'd been a damn good dad, while this woman had utterly abandoned her.

"You gone deaf?" the woman barked. "Where is my daughter? I want her."

Grace remained silent, her fury mounting. Damned if she would send this woman to a school full of kids to pull Faith out and take her God knew where. Carter needed to know Lizzie was back in town, needed to know *now*.

"How about if I get Carter on the phone?" Grace asked, striving to maintain an even tone. "You can talk to him about this."

"Like hell." The woman dropped the leather jacket, pulling a black pistol from its folds as it went down.

Grace found herself looking into the round barrel of a gun as flat black as the woman's hair. Her mouth went paper dry, her voice dying off into a tiny squeak. Fear she'd never known wedged in her throat, all from a hunk of metal with a hole in it pointed at her heart.

"Where is my daughter? Tell me now, bitch."

Nothing came from Grace's mouth. If she'd been hesitant about sending this woman to Faith's school before, she certainly wasn't going to let her go down there with a gun.

"I said *now*."

Lizzie didn't raise her voice—no chance of the guys down the hill in the stables hearing—but the words were final.

"Let me call Carter," Grace said quickly. She needed to hear his voice—not only that, Carter would call Ross, his deputy brother. "You two need to work this out."

The gun didn't waver, but Lizzie sneered. "Figures. He'd go for a snotty little soft girl like you."

"You need to go." Grace firmed her voice, like she did when her two older brothers got too bossy and obnoxious. What she wouldn't give for a chance visit from Kyle or Ray now.

"Not until you tell me where Faith is. I want my kid."

Damn it. Grace would never tell her—and anyway, what kind of woman wouldn't understand that on a school day, during the school year, her daughter would be at the elementary school in White Fork? But Lizzie wasn't from Riverbend. She'd known Carter in his gang days in Houston, and she'd come here to find him. After a brief and much gossiped about fling, she'd vanished just as quickly.

The silence went on too long. Grace saw the tightening of Lizzie's eyes and her finger on the trigger.

In that split second, Grace dove back behind the kitchen door, but not fast enough.

The sound of the shot exploded in Grace's ears, blotting out all else, except pain. Then came the bright smell of blood to overpower the warm, chocolate-cake scent of the kitchen. Grace fell to the floor, her legs no longer working.

The last thing she saw of Lizzie was the woman turning and running, a black flash in the bright sunshine. Grace heard shouting from the men at the stables, the neighing of startled horses.

Grace's limp fingers closed around the cell phone in her pocket. Her hand was all bloody, the red obscuring her contact list, so annoying. She managed to touch her thumb to the name *Carter*. Her ears still ringing from the shot, she could barely hear him answer in his rumbling, beloved voice.

"Carter," she whispered. Whatever happened after that was a blank.

End of Excerpt

Grant Campbell's
Hotter 'n' Hell Texas Chili
And its milder cousin

Makes about four servings
(a nice hearty bowl)

Ingredients

1 1/2 to 2 pounds ground beef (ground sirloin works well)

1 yellow onion, chopped (or two teaspoons of dried, minced onion)

2 cloves of garlic, minced (or two teaspoons of garlic granules)

2 4-oz cans of diced green chiles

OR 1-2 jalapeño peppers seeded and chopped

3 tablespoons chili powder (chili powder commonly found in grocery stores is fine)

2 teaspoons cumin

2 teaspoons dried oregano

1/2 teaspoon ground cayenne pepper (optional)

1-2 tablespoons specialty chile powder (depending on how hot you want it — guajillo powder, Hatch chile powder, or habanero powder — see **Note**)

2 14-oz cans of beef broth

1 cup of water (more as needed)

Salt / pepper

Warning: ALWAYS use gloves when peeling, seeding, and dicing fresh chile peppers. The juices, membranes, and seeds can seriously burn your skin.

1. Brown meat with onion, garlic, and fresh jalapeños or canned chiles (8-10 minutes).

2. Once meat is browned, transfer the meat mixture into in a Dutch oven or slow cooker. Add beef broth and 2 cups water.

3. Add chili powder, cumin, oregano, cayenne, and then specialty chile powders to taste. Mild chile powders give the chili a smoky flavor without adding too much heat. Hotter powders (e.g., habanero) crank up the heat.

If using the **Dutch oven**, simmer for two hours, covered, stirring and adding liquid as needed.

If using the **slow cooker**, cover and simmer for four hours at least, adding liquid as needed.

For both methods:

4. After one hour, taste and add another tablespoon of regular chili powder, 1/4 teaspoon cayenne (if using), and 1 teaspoon specialty chile powder.

5. Taste after another hour and add more cayenne or specialty chile powders if needed.

6. Before serving, add salt and pepper to taste.

Serve with: Cornbread and grated cheese (cheddar or Monterey Jack). A dollop of sour cream or a flour tortilla can bring down the heat for those who need it.

Milder version: Same as hot version, but use mild chile powders, and fresh or canned mild green chiles instead of jalapeños (also see **Note 2**).

Even hotter version: If you really want to turn up the heat, use fresh serrano or habanero peppers in place of jalapeños or green chiles.

Heat scale:
Scoville heat scale for chiles (approximate values)
Habanero = 200,000
Serrano = 7000-25,000
Guajillo = 5000
Jalapeño = 3500-4000
Anaheim (green) = 1000
Bell peppers = 0

Note: Specialty chile powders can be ordered from Mild Bill's in Texas (www.mildbills.com) and Native Seed Search in Tucson, Arizona (www.nativeseeds.org).

Browse their sites for varieties of chile powders. Try different powders for fun. I like the guajillo chile powder from Native Seeds, and the Hatch chile powders from Mild Bill's.

Note 2: Grant believes his chili to be a true Texas chili, which means no beans or even tomatoes. If you love tomatoes in your chili, feel free to add a can of peeled, chopped tomatoes (or peel and chop fresh ones in season). Tomatoes will also cool down the heat.

Enjoy!

Grace Malory's
Triple Chocolate-Chip
Cookies

Makes 30-40 cookies

8 tablespoons (1 stick) unsalted butter (cut into small pieces and soft but not too squishy)

1/2 cup granulated white sugar

1/2 cup firmly packed brown sugar

1 egg

1 teaspoon vanilla

2 cups all-purpose flour

1/2 teaspoon baking soda

1/2 teaspoon baking powder

1/4 teaspoon salt

White chocolate chips (about 1/3 cup)

Dark chocolate chips (about 1/3 cup)

Semi-sweet chocolate chips (about 1/3 cup)

Grease cookie sheets or use sheets of ungreased foil

Preheat oven to 375

1. Beat butter with brown and white sugars until light and fluffy, about 3-4 minutes with a handheld mixer.

2. Add egg and vanilla and beat until combined.

3. In a separate bowl, combine flour, baking soda, baking powder, and salt.

4. Add dry ingredients to butter / egg mixture all at once, and beat with electric mixer until just combined. (If dough is too wet, add another 1/8 – 1/4 cup of flour and stir by hand until combined.)

5. Stir in white chocolate, then dark, then semi-sweet chocolate chips. Add more of your favorite!

Drop about one tablespoon of dough for each cookie onto cookie sheets or foil, about 1 to 1 1/2 inches apart.

Bake in a 375 oven for 10 minutes

Transfer to wire cooling racks. Serve warm or cool.

Once cooled, store in an airtight container.

About the Author

New York Times bestselling and award-winning author Jennifer Ashley has written more than 75 published novels and novellas in romance, urban fantasy, and mystery under the names Jennifer Ashley, Allyson James, and Ashley Gardner. Her books have been nominated for and won Romance Writers of America's RITA (given for the best romance novels and novellas of the year), several *RT BookReviews* Reviewers Choice awards (including Best Urban Fantasy, Best Historical Mystery, and Career Achievement in Historical Romance), and Prism awards for her paranormal romances. Jennifer's books have been translated into more than a dozen languages and have earned starred reviews in *Booklist*.

More about Jennifer's books and series can be found at www.jenniferashley.com

Or email Jennifer at jenniferashley@cox.net

CPSIA information can be obtained at www.ICGtesting.com
Printed in the USA
LVOW10s1728091015

457650LV00006B/426/P